THE NAXALITES

THE NAXALITES

KHWAJA AHMAD ABBAS

EDITED WITH AN INTRODUCTION BY
SURESH KOHLI

NIYOGI
BOOKS

Published by
NIYOGI BOOKS
D-78, Okhla Industrial Area, Phase-I
New Delhi-110 020, INDIA
Tel: 91-11-26816301, 49327000
Fax: 91-11-26810483, 26813830
email: niyogibooks@gmail.com
website: www.niyogibooksindia.com

Cover (film poster): SMM Ausaja

Editor: Upama Biswas
Design: Shashi Bhushan Prasad

ISBN: 978-93-83098-85-9
Year of Publication: 2015

Printed at: Niyogi Offset Pvt. Ltd., New Delhi, India

CONTENTS

CONTENTS

INTRODUCTION

The journey from a written word to a cinematic experience is full of innumerable circumstantial potholes. That's probably why few have tried to tread the two grounds simultaneously. One such individual in India was Khwaja Ahmad Abbas, a self-confessed communicator of impulses, ideas, and ideologies, simultaneously operating in two mediums: films and writing. A rebel of sorts, he had announced his credo from the hallowed corridors of Aligarh Muslim University when barely after earning a law degree, he straightaway made a beeline for the 'city of dreams'—now called Mumbai. Taking up a job for pittance in Abdullah Brelvi's Bombay Chronicle, he honed his skills as a budding film critic before challenged into writing the script of a film, because he had been finding loopholes in the films he had been reviewing. The challenge resulted in Bombay Talkies' *Naya Sansar*, starring Ashok Kumar in the role of a journalist, which turned out to be a silver jubilee hit.

Long years later when his short and long fiction indulgences started to appear in print he would often be propelled by the question of identity, because he had, by then, begun to ride in not one, not two, but three boats: journalism, creative writing and scriptwriting for films. And succeeding in all three fields, his prompt answer was: "When I am making a film I am fascinated by writing, and when I am writing I am fascinated by films. I think this division gives one relaxation."

Often dubbed as someone who saw tomorrow yesterday, as almost all his later films seem to indicate, *The Naxalites* being one, he stands true to this label in his description of the film, in an interview to the *Indian Literary Review*, in the following words:

"I'm making The Naxalites – a very dangerous film. I feel scared of being shot at from both sides, though I think it is neither a glorification nor a denigration of the Naxalites. I only hope that the film is not misunderstood as my story *Sardarji* was. ...I was excited by these people who were willing to do or die, to kill or die. And I said to myself that here is a great drama... A great human drama if the people can be so motivated and so dedicated to an ideal that they will kill or be killed. I thought it would be worth analysing and also because I had a theory of my own, which might be purely subjective, that this thing is rooted in the Bengal Famine of 1943, that the first Naxalites were babies at that time and that in their subconsciousness lurked the bitterness of Calcutta pavements. That is what I have tried to show in this film."

The film eventually got made with a lot of compromises: shortage of finances, lack and absence of star dates being some of them. Also by this time Mithun Chakravarty had crossed the *lakshman rekha* between art and mainstream cinema, and so had Smita Patil, though that had not been the reason for the casting of the two. Mithun had been cast because he had been a part of the Naxal movement, and Smita, because of her sympathy for the downtrodden.

One need not delve into the growth of this extreme left movement after the break-up of Communist Party of India (CPM)–

splitting into two separate political parties in 1967 in a West Bengal village called Naxalbari, later finding further stronghold in different southern and eastern parts of the country, particularly Andhra Pradesh, Odisha, Chhatisgarh and, of course, pockets of West Bengal. The turning point of the violent movement (aimed at eliminating the haves for the survival of the have-nots) was when school and college students abandoned education and joined the movement. The rest is living history. There are many, however, who associate the genesis of the movement to the 1942-43 Bengal famine. The famine being yet another subject on which Abbas had attempted a cinematic neo-realistic adventure, in the form of *Dharti ke Laal,* which has since, reportedly, become an essential text in the syllabi of the Film & Television Institute of India, Pune.

Since Abbas's novel and film, the subject has in some form or the other found its way into not only novels and short stories in various Indian languages but also several cinematic attempts, to draw attention to the movement. The subject has provided impetus for both individuals converting to the 'cause' as well as semi-biopics, such as *Maathaad Maathaadu Mallige* and *Thalappavu* (Malayalam), *Sindhooram* (Telegu), *Veerappa Nayaka* (Kannada), *Ko* (Tamil), *Swayamsiddha* (Oriya), *Eka Nakshalwadya Cha Janma* (Marathi), *Hazaar Chaurasi ki Maa, Hazaron Khwaishein Aisi, Tango Charlie, Chamku, Red Alert: The War Within, Chakravyuh* (Hindi), to name some that instantly come to mind.

The Naxalites does not just pay mere lip service but also draws attention to, however minimally, the failure of the State along with the Fourth Estate agencies to ensure at least the basic common denominators like shelter, drinking water, food, sanitation, employment, proper wages; questionable judiciary, self-centric bureaucracy, rampant corruption, misuse of ill-gotten wealth and its vulgar display, the inhuman approach of law enforcing agencies–aspects the parameters of which have continued to be on the up. In film after film, especially from *Char Dil Char Rahen* onwards, Abbas raised issues that have a direct bearing on the existence of the have-nots, whose ultimate weapon is protest (that sometimes takes the form of a violent movement), and the State's indifference to their demands.

Being a socially conscious individual (he lived in a rented accommodation till the end), both the scripts Abbas wrote for others and the films made under the Naya Sansar banner gave vent to that commitment. All inessential romantic, song-and-dance interludes have remained conspicuous by their absence from Abbas's movies; even when he did deploy them, they were never allowed to dilute the narrative flow as is otherwise manifested in mainstream commercial cinema. What counted for him was his message.

While Mithun Chakravorty (it was his second coming after Mrinal Sen's *Mrigaya* for which also he won the coveted National Award) and Smita Patil led the cast of *The Naxalites*, all others had been drawn from his regular stable–Nana Palsikar, Imtiaz Khan (elder brother of Amjad Khan), Tinnu Anand (son of his best friend, writer Inder Raj Anand) as a manual rickshaw puller, his wife Pushi Anand (Shahnaz; daughter of old-time actor-comedian Agha) as a foreign newspaper columnist, and Jalal Agha (a must in every Abbas venture, brother of Pushi Anand) as a tribal. Even yours truly had been invited to be part of a scene but couldn't make it in time to tinsel town to be counted amongst those who fell to police bullets. Shot at authentic locations, to the extent possible, the film had the reformed Naxalite essaying the role of a homeless grave-dweller who is constantly nagged by the memories of his mother prostituting for survival in Kolkata bylanes; and it is while watching *Dharti ke Laal* that he literally turns hysterical relating to happenings on the screen. On release, critics unanimously panned it mercilessly, though it will remain a crucial expressionist audio-video document when everything gets archived.

A posting about the film on the net goes like this:

> "K A Abbas is a true visionary and his movies reflect the deprivations and vicissitudes of Indian masses, so don't watch this (*The Naxalites*) if you don't have stomach to watch a man being tortured as an ashtray by the cops with cigarette butts, famished peasants wondering in the lush green Bengal as they drop dead, a man selling his mother on the street as a whore, an orphan living in a grave in a cemetery, for these are the soulful but wrathful images which fill the screen in a requiem for the great Bengali nation in quest for their aspirations and deliverance in this veracious drama."

Almost all ventures made under the Naya Sansar returned the monies invested in them. Kobita Sarkar summed it beautifully in her essay "Film Maker with a Message", where she observed:

> "Part of the reason again for his lack of commercial success is because he falls between two tools of not making enough concessions to the popular urge for the tawdry, and the one of his overstating his obsessive comment, which diminishes the attraction of his films for the more critically sophisticated. With constantly changing audiences, it is near-impossible feat to acquire a finely measured balance. A re-assessment of how much moral uplift an audience can take without boredom or embarrassment is called for."

Abbas in both his writings and in his cinema refused to glorify or romanticise reality, even though at times the subject or situations warranted it; and that's why he remained diminished in both forms of creative communication. From simply a writer he was lured into being a producer and director of his own films after the phenomenal success of *Awaara,* a movie for which he had written the script, with the reworking of the same theme of environment and hereditary and with Nargis essaying a double role opposite Raj Kapoor in the first home production, *Anhonee*. Unlike other films he scripted for the RK Banner both *Mera Naam Joker* and *Bobby* had been written as novels in the first place and the same had been the case with *The Naxalites*.

Reverting to the somewhat euphoric essay on the net the earlier quoted unabashed indulger in sycophancy observed:

> "K. A. Abbas was possibly the most definitive and progressive activist in Indian literature and cinema. He is an intellectual who tries to redeem and solve a paradox without making a crucial issue into pseudo-intellectual paradigm, his personal life akin to his public profile is affiliated with his passion for his causes versus the eponymous vitriolic opposition of his critics."

All Abbas attempted as a communicator of ideas was in one way or another aimed at highlighting the right, the truth, as he perceived it to be, in order to arouse the conscience of the man in the street, not to incite him into rebellion, but to assuage him from adopting confrontationist tendencies, to protest, to demand that is rightfully his and get it by peaceful means. The humanist in him silently suffered but never stopped short of rising against it. In story after story, in script after script, in column after column, in essay after essay, and in novel after novel his philosophy is that of a quiet rebel against every authority that countered his conscience. As was, for instance, evident when he challenged the State's censoring authority and fought to the bitter end in the Supreme Court of India, in defence of what he had sought to show in his documentary *A Tale of Four Cities*, eventually getting the orders reversed in his favour.

Montage is a technique Abbas deployed in all his creative expressions—a juxtaposition of images to integrate the imagined into the real—for he strongly believed, though not necessarily always correctly, that the best way to draw attention to a malady was, "when delusive wish-fulfillment littered the screen", arguably, the most prominent example being *The Naxalites* text as well.

Simplicity of expression and sincerity of purpose has been the mainstay of all of Khwaja Ahmad Abbas's writings. There is no denying the fact that his writings are grossly affected by Leftist, Communist leanings, through which his social vision views all aspects of life. When he wrote a novel or a short story, his subconscious would be alive to the possibilities of visual treatments, but while converting them into cinematic interpretations he failed to leave out ground realities and sought to bring them alive in their grimness. The narrative of *The Naxalites* is both straightforward and anecdotal, nothing mendacious yet not without the necessary leverage or license in telling a story that was rooted in the circumstantial.

Unlike in the printed form, cinema is limited in both length and natural time zone. While a novel can be expanded to any length, its cinematic interpretation or depiction is time bound and cannot by any means contain all the different stories and situations. Regardless of the time one visits a cinema theatre to watch, re-watch and enjoy the story(ies) unfold on the giant screen, every reading of a good or great novel opens up fresh vistas and newer stories. Many classics have failed to result in great or absorbing cinematic interpretation but there have been films that have immortlised many ordinary literary works down the years. Cinema is spectacular, and so is its impact, but a novel or a story in itself cannot be.

Despite sincerity of purpose *The Naxalites* failed to arouse excitement as a film, but then that does not in any way diminish its impact in the narrative form.

Suresh Kohli

February 2015

HE MADE ME A NAXALITE AGAIN

"My name had reached Bombay before I could. People in the industry, and outside it, knew all about my involvement with the Naxalite movement in Calcutta and my close links with Charu Mazumdar, the fiery leader of the Naxalites. I had quit the movement after there was a tragedy in my family, but the label of being a Naxalite moved with me wherever I went, whether it was the FTII in Poona or when I came to Bombay in the late seventies...

I was trying my best to forget the past when the renowned writer and filmmaker Khwaja Ahmad Abbas found me and told me that he was making a film about the Naxalite movement called *The Naxalites*, and wanted me to lead the cast. I almost decided not to do the film because I knew it would remind me of those troublesome days and nights running away from the Police all the time, and facing the risk of death any time. But, it was the name of Abbas Sahab that inspired me to do the film. I was being branded as a dancer and a fighter more than an actor, and it was the chance of playing a Naxalite in a film directed by Abbas Sahab that made me accept the challenge of "living" the life of a Naxalite again. The other big temptation was the opportunity of working with a fantastic actress like Smita Patil, who was also totally involved in the making of the film...

It is more than thirty-four years since the film was made, but I will always remember it as one of the most memorable films of my career. More than anything, I was fascinated by the man called K.A. Abbas. I had only heard about him at the FTII and knew that he was the writer of some great films made by Raj Kapoor, and had made his own films which were very different from the run-of-the-mill films made in Bombay. But it was a mind-blowing experience coming in touch with such a simple man with such high values of life, and his own simple ways of working as a writer and a filmmaker...

He was, I remember, a very hard taskmaster and tried his best to get the best of the actors working with him. He gave Smita and me a narration of the script and asked us if we had any questions. We had no questions at all. We were willing to do anything he asked. Once we had agreed to work in the film, we had to follow all his instructions and orders, called in his strong voice, a kind of voice which we had never heard. He made it very clear that he would not be able to pay us the price we asked other filmmakers. We worked free for him, but I remember that he still handed over cheques of some amount to both Smita and me...

He told us that we would not have all the fancy clothes because they did not go with our characters. He also took us by surprise when he said there would be no personal make-up man or hairdresser for us and no conveyance money. We had to agree, because we knew it was his way of working; big stars, who worked in his films, did the same. He even asked us to travel second class or third class by train from Bombay to Calcutta, for the shooting. We all shared the same food and ate at the same table. Abbas Sahab, as we had heard, was like any common man, but had the mind of a philosopher who knew human psychology very well...

The film was a great attempt to capture the spirit of the Naxalite movement, but like all his other films, it did not do well at the box-office. For me, however, it was a great experience working with a man who was an example of "simple living and high thinking" at its best...

I met him after *The Naxalites* a couple of times, but never saw him sitting idle. He was a man on the move, and was like that till the end of his life. I have worked with some of the greatest filmmakers, but Abbas Sahab was one of his kind. I salute the great man and will always remember him and his last words to me in which he had said that I would be a big star one day, and that when it happened I should not let success go to my head but be of use to the people and the workers of the industry. And fortunately for me, I am doing just that as my tribute to Abbas Sahab or that is what I feel as the leader of the workers, taking up their cause with the sincere care and affection I have for them. I have been doing as much as I can for the welfare of these workers who have so much faith in me. I wish a man like Abbas Sahab was around now to see what I am today and what I am doing..."

Mithun Chakravorty

(Courtesy: Ali Peter John)

All characters—and incidents—in this novel (and in the screenplay on which it is based) are fictitious, but none is entirely imaginary.

Time: 1967-76

PROLOGUE
THIRD EYE OF SHIVA

"That is the third eye of Shiva," said Comrade Dada, as a spotlight was suddenly focused upon them, piercing the all-pervading darkness of the jungle.

"That is the symbol of destruction. So, be ready to kill or to die. *Bus*," he chopped the air with his hand. "*Khalas*! But you are not to fire the first shot. Wait for *them* to begin."

The glare of the spotlight lit up the faces of the young men, and some young women too-crouching beside him.

There on his right was Ajoy Bose, the journalist, whom he had once thought of as just a playboy in silken *khadi*, bush shirt and trousers. But here was Ajoy beside him, loyal in the hour of decision.

To his left was Kamala Sen, smart of face and slim of figure, who had come to join the Naxalites, with powder and lipstick on her face. He had mocked her for her appearance. "That is not what a girl who is going to be dedicated to revolution should look like!" But what else could be expected of a Congress leader's daughter. It was good that, she had come to them from such a family! "So you are Mukul Babu's daughter," he had said, remembering the friend of his youth.

Mukul, his class-fellow in school, used to call him "Shoka"– short form of Ashoka!

And he would call him Motu Muku, for Mukul was chubby even then. Both of them had played football together–Motu Muku was the obvious goalkeeper (his body would fill the goal-post– there would be no space for the ball to go through!–That's why he would always teasingly throw at Mukul). Ashoke Mazumdar, with his thin legs, was always the centre-forward–"With your speed, you will go very far." How very far–in what direction?–they had no idea–his team-members would always say. He chuckled to himself at the memory.

They had both donned Gandhi caps and marched in Congress processions led by the fiery Subhas Chandra Bose, their idol and ideal of those days.

They were both arrested and imprisoned together in the Civil Disobedience Movement. They were both Gandhities then. But in prison, they were both a nuisance to the jail authorities. So the jailor decided to separate them. He transferred Ashoke Mazumdar, the lean and bespectacled one, to another ward, thereby setting into motion the cycle of incidents and influences which would transform a non-violent Gandhite into a violent Naxalite eventually. But the transformation was not immediate and he would take many decades to arrive at this spot in the jungle on the border of Bengal and Bihar.

It had been a pilgrimage of sorts–though he had given up religion on the way–from Nehruism to Congress Socialism, under the influence of the fiery and fire-eating Doctor Ram Manohar Lohia, whose anti-Nehruism was an inverted form of his former Nehru-worship. From that to the Communist Party, under the mild Puran Chandra Joshi, was the logical step. When the split finally came, he joined hands with Ranadive and Jyoti

Basu, and EMS Namboodiripad of Kerala, and became a Marxist Communist. But he was ever on a leftward move and when the Marxists went into the United Front, he and Charu Mazumdar formed the Marxist-Leninist-Maoist Party which, because of its first revolutionary action in the village around Naxalbari, came to be popularly known as the Naxalite movement. He had been called "Comrade Dada" for so long, that he had almost forgotten his original name!

"I hope their leader—Comrade Dada—is also here!" grimly thought the DIG—Reserve Police (anti-Naxalite branch), Gangooly, as the third eye of his searchlight, mounted on his weapon-carrier, probed the jungle.

He had old scores to settle with Comrade Dada. It was Dada who had enticed his only son, Anand, into the poisonous coils of his Naxalite movement and then, one day, wantonly killed him—or he had had him killed by a girl, who had fired a pistol, at point-blank range, into his son's face. The face that he used to kiss and fondle, the face that was still smooth and babyish, without even the growth of the beard darkening the soft curves. It was only on his last birthday that he had presented him his first safety razor to shave down the soft shadowy that had covered his cheeks, and which needed at least a weekly shave. Yet that hard-hearted demon of a girl had killed him—what was her name?

Yes, it was Ajitha. And he was satisfied to know that, after years of her trial and prosecution and various legal procrastinations, she had been hanged last month.

"She shot my son without mercy," he reflected now, "and it was only justice that she got the gallows. Why should I spare my tears for her?" And yet, when they read the news of her hanging in the papers, his wife was crying. These women are impossible! Crying over the hanging of the murderess of her son! He would not spare a tear for the death of a Naxalite. Yet when he looked into the mirror he saw the moisture of tears in his own eyes. Why? Was it because it was said along the grapevine that Anand the Ajitha were supposed to be in love! Love and Hate! They were two faces of the same coin. He had dearly loved his son, the young Anand, whom, he had affectionately called Annoo.

Now that a Naxalite named Ajitha had killed his Annoo, he hunted them all–all the Naxalites–wherever they went they brought with them death and destruction, hatred and violence–so he had sublimated his own personal sorrow at the death of a son into a holy crusade, and volunteered to join the Anti-Naxalite School as an instructor where he was to teach policemen and police officers to hate Naxalites–and to exterminate them! Since his son's death, that was the mission of his life. And today he had surrounded and would kill all of them–and their leader!

"Take it easy, Khan Saheb," said Comrade Dada to the incongruous Pathan in baggy shalwar who was aiming his deadly long rifle directly at the flashlight. "Not yet, not yet! Let them begin the fireworks. Then shoot to your heart's content. Fire, *and* fire–till the last bullet is exhausted. *Khatam karo ya khatam hojao*!" He again chopped the air with his right hand, the fanatical gesture, which had brought the death warrant to so many Naxalites and non-Naxalites. The leader had no mercy for the enemies of the people–and that included even Naxalites who were even vaguely suspected to be police informers, or less than rigid in their devotion to the "Party" and the cause of "Revolution". They were expendable and, therefore, they were doomed!

"You are doomed, Naxalites. You are surrounded on all sides," came the voice of DIG Gangooly over the loudspeaker from the police van, as he took the microphone in his hand. He spat out venom and his voice, magnified, was like the voice of doom in that jungly wilderness. "There is no escape for you. You have to surrender–raise both your hands to show you have thrown away your arms and are ready to be arrested..."

Behind the barricade...

The arrow in the taut bow in the hands of the dark-bodied Kanu Santhal, tribal turned Naxalite, behind whom crouched his four-year-old son, Surya, was poised for flight, aimed directly at the blinking, blinding searchlight.

Suddenly Comrade Dada's hand gently pressed his shoulder and he relaxed his taut bow and arrow.

By his side was the equally dark Andhra, Raghoo, the ex-rickshaw driver, who was aiming his double-barreled gun, peeping through the shrubs and branches piled over the barricade. His finger was on the trigger, but he also obeyed Comrade Dada's gesture to hold back the fire for the time being.

"Naxalites!" came Gangooly's voice from across the dark gap separating the weapons-carrier and the barricade. "Why don't you show your faces? Why are you hiding like womenfolk? Come out, you cowards!"

"Cowards!" That is what he had called them. That was too much for Kanu Santhal, the dark Adivasi, to bear. And the arrow left his bow, directly aimed at the lens of the flashlight. There was a shattering of glass as the arrow found its mark, and in the sudden darkness in which both sides were plunged, two voices were heard.

"Fire!" ordered Gangooly's voice.

"*Khatam kar do–ya khatam hojao!*" came the answering command of Comrade Dada.

After that the darkness was split by the flash of guns and rifles and revolvers.

In the dim starlight, the hole in the barrel of the service revolver looked like a blind eye. When the trigger was pressed there was a flash and a report. The flash illuminated the handsome but gaunt features of DIG Gangooly in the protective shadow of the weapons-carrier.

On the other side, also in dim starlight, the two blind eyes of a double-barreled gun protruded through the leaves and branches. There was a flash and a report. The flash illuminated the grim but youthful face of Amar Kaal, hiding behind a tree in the jungle barricade.

The long muzzle of a machine gun protruded through the bushes. There was a series of flashes, as the ominous chatter of a machine gun was heard. The flash revealed the profile of a police officer.

Three Naxalites were hit by the machine-gun fire and fell down in the agony of death.

The extra-long barrel of the Pathan's muzzle-loading gun was creeping along, aimed at the distant "chattering" machine gun. The report and the flash illuminated the grim aquiline profile of Haibat Khan, the Pathan. But the smile on his lips as he found his aim, was extinguished by a police machine-gun bullet. With an "*Allaho Akbar*" he breathed his last.

The police officer manning the machine gun was hit by the bullet fired by Haibat Khan, but another police officer took his place and his machine gun while the wounded officer was moved backwards.

"Machine gun *chalao*," came the command of the DIG.

The new machine-gunner pressed the trigger, and in the flashes he was seen moving the lethal weapon from left to right.

Two Naxalites—Sinha and Anwarul Haq were knocked down by the machine-gun fire. Dr Ashraf Ali picked up the gun of one of his fallen comrades with grim determination, inserted a cartridge in the breach of the barrel and aimed it through the branches at the police across the barricade. He pressed the trigger, in the flash were illuminated the grim but handsome features of the doctor, ironically enough, who was today taking lives instead of saving lives.

A police officer was struck down by the bullet from the doctor's gun, but he was immediately replaced by two other policemen.

Kanu Santhal, the sturdy, broad-chested tribal, picked up his bow and arrow again and aimed his arrow at the chattering and flashing machine gun.

Suddenly a new searchlight was switched on and the circle of light fell on Kanu as he was about to release the arrow. A machine-gun bullet fired directly at him got him in the chest but the arrow was released and was in flight. Kanu fell down dead. The flashlight moved on, he was just a dark, dead body, his son by his side crying "Baba—Baba!"

The arrow had hit one of the machine-gunners who was pierced through the arm. He was taken back and another replacement took his place.

Rummaging through her *jhola*, Kamala Sen came upon two hand grenades which she hurled at the police party, with a shout of "*Inqilab Zindabad*". They burst ineffectively in the centre of the no man's land between the two barricades. She herself was caught in the moving circle of light, and was shot down.

But the explosion was the excuse that the DIG was waiting for.

He bellowed, "They are throwing bombs at us. Finish them–exterminate them."

The machine guns chattered again and more ominously, and a howitzer was brought into action.

The burst of the howitzer shell was the climax of this grim, bloody dialogue between two inexorable forces–the arrogant force of "law and order" at all cost, and the impatient ballations of "instant revolution"!

Comrade Dada–alias Ashoke Mazumdar–called Shoka by the friends of his childhood—was the last of them to die. His last words were "*Khatam kar do–ya khatam ho jao!*" and his last gesture was to chop the air with his left hand. But he was midway in his gesture when his end came. "*Khatam kar do-ya khatam...*" That was his last word and his epitaph–*khatam*!

For a moment there was a ceasefire–and eerie silence–and darkness–the jungle sounds came to life–crickets chirping, frogs croaking, birds fluttering their feathers, before taking off on their pre-dawn flight.

A searchlight was switched on. Silhouetted by it, DIG Gangooly took a long list in his hand and started calling out all the names of the NAXALITES...

The circle of light moved from face to face till it was focused on the dead face of Amar Kaal...

"Amar Kaal! Amar Kaal!" DIG Gangooly called twice.

I

THE MAN WHO LIVED IN A GRAVE

Amar Kaal was his unusual name. His habitation was just as peculiar. He lived in a grave—a Christian grave in an old, and now disused, British cemetery off Park Circus.

Amar Kaal was brought up in cosmopolitan but famine-ridden Calcutta, and condemned in his childhood to begging from British Tommies, American GI's, Sikh jawans and Marwari businessmen, as well as the Bengali *bhadralok*. He had a workable knowledge of spoken Bengali, Hindi, and even a smattering of some words of English. For the last fifteen years, he had been a protégé of Uncle Johnny, the old caretaker of the cemetery—till his death and burial in a common man's grave in another cemetery.

His remains could not be accommodated in this vast place that, all his life, he had tended with such loving care, sweeping the dry leaves from the tombstones, keeping the door locked, keeping out the homeless beggars, and the criminals who might have made it their hideout. This was one of the inexplicable facts of life—why Uncle Johnny's remains could not be interred in this cemetery. But now that Uncle Johnny was gone, he had left the whole cemetery as an undisputed legacy to Amar Kaal and even the padres did not mind his living there, so long as he did not pester them for Uncle Johnny's pension. So he was the undisputed master of this vast courtyard with its protective boundary walls, its tombs and its mausoleums. Some of them had not been used, and served him well as a protection against the sun and the monsoons, and cold wintry winds.

Amar Kaal! Why had his mother or father given him this name? He often wondered as he lay down to sleep. He had asked one of the artists who sometimes came to the cemetery to make some sketches and the artist told him it was the oddest name that he had heard. Why was he called Amar Kaal which meant, "Long Live Famine"?

"Maybe," the artist had replied, "But do you remember something about your father and mother?"

"No, Sir–I don't remember anything. I have been an orphan always!"

That answer about not remembering anything about his mother and father was not strictly true.

Could one call them memories–or should one call them *sapnay*–dreams? Or just thoughts that came into the mind, haphazardly, from God knows where? But he could not share them with a stranger, however kind he might be. He would think him mad. And then *they*–the police–would send him to the *pagal khana*, the madhouse where the crazy ones lived! Was he crazy?

This thought often troubled him, and once again it was troubling him on that night which lay over the cemetery like a silken sheet of peace! He would have dozed off to sleep with the question still unresolved when a voice from outside disturbed him.

"*Ma*–" somebody was saying and the word stunned him to the core like an electric wire which he had once, by mistake, touched.

"*Ma-dar*–." That is the commonest word of abuse that one hears twenty times a day on any street of any city in India but to Amar Kaal, it was a personal insult and a personal challenge.

He rushed out of the grave that served him as a bedroom.

Like a monkey he climbed the boundary wall of the cemetery. Outside under the street lamp, two men and a veiled woman were standing.

The pimp—he looked like a *dalla*, he was sure–was talking to the veiled woman, pointing to the white-dhotied *bhadralok* customer beside him, "*Babuji bees rupaye dega–Das rupaye tumhare–Das rupaye meray! Bus hogaya saudah!*"

Amar Kaal shouted to the pimp, "*Kiyon bay*–selling your mother! You scoundrel!" And, to back his words, he threw a stone which fell with an ominous thud at the feet of the pimp. The customer and the pimp both jumped at this rude intrusion.

Seeing an approaching policeman, the pimp heaved a sigh of relief. "*Havildar Saheb, Havildar Saheb*! This man, here, is interfering with my business."

The policeman interrogated him from the pavement.

"What's your name?"

"Amar Kaal!" came the reply.

"What sort of name is that?"

"That is the name my mother gave me."

"Where do you live?"

The man on the wall pointed to the tombs behind him.

"I live in a grave."

"What's that?" The policeman reacted as if he had been interrogating a ghost.

"Am I breaking a law by living in a grave?"

The policeman nodded, "Well, if the padres don't mind. But why did you disturb this gentlemen here?"

"He was selling his mother–so I stopped him from doing that!"

The policeman took another line of reasoning. "He might be selling *his* mother. Why should you mind? After all, he was not selling *your* mother?"

At that, the man on the boundary wall jumped down and pounced on the policeman, catching him by the collar of his uniform shirt.

"How dare you talk about my mother?" he shrieked between grimly clenched teeth, "I will kill you!"

As he pressed the throat of the policeman with his fingers, the whistle in the policeman's mouth blew of itself–the exhaled breath passing through it.

Two other policemen came running to their colleague's rescue. Finding a ruffian attacking a policeman, they grabbed the man and pulled him away from his stranglehold on the pot-bellied havildar.

"Attacking a policeman!" the havildar shouted now that he was free. "Take him away to the police station!"

As Amar Kaal was led away, the havildar was greeted by the obsequious pimp. "May you live long, *Havildar Saheb*, to protect us–respectable traders, from these ruffians who take the law in their own hands!" Saying this he pressed a five-rupee currency note into the havildar's palm.

"That's all right!" pronounced the havildar, "You carry on your trade without any botheration. Let me know if any one makes trouble for you. I will put him straight."

"Thank you, Sir," said the pimp, *salaming* the havildar. Then he turned to the babu in white.

"There you are, Sir. Now you make a night of it with this girl and good luck to you. That will be twenty rupees, Sir." He extended his palm but it remained empty.

"Some other time," replied the would-be customer, "Tonight I have been put off by that crazy fellow on the wall!" Then he sauntered away.

The pimp tried to take the disappointment in his stride. He gallantly turned to the veiled girl. "Don't worry, my dear! There are hundreds of such babus in the city. I'll find another one for you right away."

"No," said the girl, "Don't worry finding another customer. I will not go with him tonight or any night. Didn't you hear what that crazy one called me?"

"What did he call you?" asked the perplexed pimp.

"He called me his mother," said the girl, and then walked away with decisive steps, resounding on the stones of the pavement.

The not-so-young man in a red *banian* and ragged jeans that must have been blue at one time, was now in a police court.

"Your name?" asked the magistrate who was already tired of all the disreputable characters paraded before him every morning.

"Amar Kaal." Came the reply from the dock as the man in the ragged red T-shirt directly faced the magistrate.

"What sort of name is that?" asked the man of law.

"Sir, this is the name that my mother gave me when I was born. It was the year of the great famine and I suppose she gave me this name so that I should never forget the famine, and I haven't!"

"Where do you live?" the magistrate continued with his interrogation.

"In a grave in the British cemetery," came the reply.

"In a grave!" asked the magistrate.

"Yes, Sir, for a number of years, I slept there peacefully. It's the only place where once can sleep without trouble. If I slept on a park bench, the police harassed me. If I slept on the footpath, the *mastaans* would demand money from me–and I had no money."

This remark provoked the interest of a journalist sitting in the court. What sort of prisoner was this? He looked up from his notes and stared hard at the man in the dirty T-shirt.

"Why did you assault the policeman?"

"I only caught him by the throat, Sir, because he was abusing my mother!" said the man in the dock.

The magistrate, anxious to end the case, gave his judgment "Now that the accused has confessed his crime, we fine him fifty rupees, or in default 15 days rigorous imprisonment."

"Fifteen days in jail, Sir? Thank you, Sir," the prisoner was almost jubilant. "I will have rest and peace at last."

"Sir," the journalist was now on his feet, "If you will allow me, Sir, I would like to pay the fine on behalf of the accused."

The *rasgullas* were sweet and juicy, and Amar Kaal wanted to eat them all together.

They–the journalist and Amar Kaal–were sitting in a restaurant near the court.

"*Babuji*," asked Amar Kaal, "why did you spend full fifty rupees to get me released?"

"Because I want your story–" replied the journalist whose name was Ajoy Bose.

"My story!" exclaimed Amar Kaal, "Would someone be interested in my story?"

"Yes, many people will be interested in your story."

"My parents died in the great famine along with hundreds of thousands. And I sleep in a grave. Does that make a story?"

"Yes, for my sort of newspaper, it does!"

"Will you take my photo also?" He asked eagerly, pointing to the camera that was lying on the table.

"Yes—but not here. In the cemetery, near *your* grave!"

The tombstone of some old pillar of the East India Company provided a strange contrast to the grim story that Amar Kaal related with some humour and much relish. He also acted the parts that he played in his life.

First he was a refugee child scrounging in the dustbin in front of the Grand Hotel, immensely hungry, prepared to eat anything and everything, with his long red tongue out of his teeth.

"*Babuji*, first I would pick out the bits of meat and bones from the dustbin full of leftovers in front of the Grand Hotel. I would keep an early morning vigil for the sweepers to emerge and empty the slops of the kitchen leftover in the dustbin, and the moment their back was turned I would pounce on them like a hungry dog. I had to fight the cats and rats and even dogs for pieces of meat and bones—beef or pork or mutton, it did not matter to me, for I had no religion except the religion of hunger. Once I heard an old mad man watching me in this free-for-all and saying, "I thought Man had descended from the apes. But now I know our ancestors were not monkeys, but wild dogs!"

Now he switched to being a beggar, supplicating before English Tommies and American GI's. He spoke pidgin English or American!—"No mother, no father—me hungry Indian boy—will pray Almighty *Gawd* for your *viktari*, *Saheb*—give me four annas *bukhsheesh*."

His hand was now pitifully extended in such an imitation of a beggar-child that Ajoy Bose had to resist putting his hand in his pocket and giving him twenty-five paise.

Then his manner and tone changed. "*Babuji*, a child could get a few pice out of the charitable–but when I grew up, the door of charity suddenly closed on me. So I had to take the help of a knife."

Now he was a *goonda* with an open knife in his hand. "Come on, you bastard! ..." He spoke through the corner of his mouth and the look on his face was so ferocious that, for a moment, Ajoy was frightened of him. "Come on, out with it, you f–g bastard!" The way eventually led me to jail and once, when I came out, an old Christian, who was caretaker, gave me new life among all these dead Englishmen. He got a lot to eat–so many Christian households would give him bread, butter, meat and vegetables–and what he got he shared with me. He was the caretaker of this cemetery–Uncle Johnny, they all called him–when he died, he gave me this cemetery as his son and heir–that's all my story–now, do you think someone would be interested in it?"

"Yes, certainly–it will be my business to make it interesting to all my readers–but tell me again, why did you throw stones at that pimp?"

"Because he was selling his *mother*" spontaneously replied Amar Kaal.

"And why did you hit out at the havildar?"

"Because he was abusing my *mother*."

"But," Ajoy gently argued with him, "Your mother is dead. And no one can abuse dead people."

"Dead or alive, my mother is my mother. Didn't you see in the *fillum Maa Qasam*, how the hero beats up the villain when he abuses his dead mother!"

Ajoy Bose was getting an idea. He asked Amar Kaal, "Do you like to see films?"

"Yes, I like *fillums*–especially those with *dhishoom-dhishoom* in them."

"Then will you come along and see a film with me?"

"Sure. Is there much *dhishoom-dhishoom* in it?"

"No–but you will get another kind of enjoyment in it."

"All right, for your sake, I will see even this film."

The film which Ajoy Bose took Amar Kaal to see was an old picture, called *Dharti Ke Lal* which was screened as the part of a festival of old films called "Nostalgia".

But it was not a pleasant nostalgia–it revived memories of the great Bengal famine of 1943 and recreated the atmosphere of those days, how one peasant family, driven by starvation, had to migrate to Calcutta, along with thousands of peasant families.

The city-bred Amar Kaal was not interested in a film showing village life. Somehow the rural details disturbed him. So when, after the titles which he could not read, he saw the scenes in a village hut, he closed his eyes and said to Ajoy, "Wake me up–if there is *dhishoom-dhishoom*." Within a few minutes he was asleep. But when the scene of Hunger March began and the background music assumed a stridently melancholy tune, he tentatively opened his eyes. On the screen thousands of peasants from the village were crawling like ants towards the city. He sat awake. When had he seen this scene before? In his dreams, of course! Then at the fag end of this caravan of destitutes he saw a dark little urchin in rage, lost, looking about for his parents, and a glimmer of recognition came into his eyes. "That's me!" He shouted aloud, nudging Ajoy Bose.

"Sh...sh...shshsh..." hissed a member of the Film Society from behind him.

Now, he saw all attention to the shadows on the silver screen.

The peasant family was now on the footpaths of Calcutta, with the men and women piteously whining, "*Mago, phan do.*"

This cry, too, he felt he had heard before. But where? In his dreams? Or in his subconscious?

Then the baby was lying on the pavement, crying piteously, and seeing it he cried again, "That's me."

"Sh sh sh sh"—again hissed the irate member of the Film Society whose evening was spoilt by this man's incoherent remarks.

When Amar Kaal saw the baby's mother, again he could feel the sting of memory in his heart. "That's my mother," he nudged Ajoy again.

"That's not your mother but a famous actress who, by her acting, is depicting what happened to your mother and thousands of other women during the famine!" explained Ajoy in whispers.

By now the young woman had left the hungry baby lying on the footpaths, and was (reluctantly, though, that Amar Kaal could see) accompanying the pimp.

Suddenly Amar Kaal got up with a frenzied movement, "No, no, this is *my* mother. Ma, Ma!" He cried out, while his huge black shadow fell on the screen, and there were shouts of protest from the spectators, as Amar Kaal shouted, "Don't go with this evil man, I will kill him. I will kill this bastard, I will..." And he marched, with a grim expression, towards the screen which his shadow now covered completely.

It was dark on the psychiatrist's couch. The sedative which she had injected put Amar Kaal under twilight sleep—so that he was asleep as well as awake.

"What do you remember of your childhood?"

Amar Kaal smiled. His first memory was of a green expanse like the green sari the psychiatrist was wearing.

But soon this green was snatched away from him like a toy taken out of a child's hands and smashed on the ground.

Cracks appeared on the toy—on the earth—on that ants were moving—no, they were not ants, they were human beings—derelicts from the villages—ultimately the crowd of ants or humans became one little, lost boy—the dark boy from the film—

Now everything was bathed in red light. Or was it only the red portrait of Che Guevara on the wall of the psychiatrist's clinic.

Now everything is green again—the green of the paddy fields—the rice crop is waving in the breeze—and Amar Kaal has a strange feeling of homecoming—

The white light was switched on—now Amar Kaal, still half-conscious, could see the handsome features of the woman psychiatrist (though he did not know who she was). She helped him to rise from his couch and led him, like a child (he thought: she has the touch of my mother), as she brought him to the huge table on which Ajoy Bose was idly thumbing through some Bengali magazines.

"Such cases are rare," said the psychiatrist, "but I have seen some at least. He has a "mother fixation". The mother's lap was snatched from him in childhood, since then he has been hankering for it. Even in the grave he finds a substitute for his mother's lap. That's why he sleeps there in peace. He finds both peace and security which he has missed since he lost his mother."

"But what about the violent reaction he had while watching *Dharti Ke Lal?*" The journalist asked, and then added, "He became violent, almost went mad."

"That, too, is a symptom of his psychological disease. His subconscious holds him responsible for his mother's downfall and, eventually, for her death!" From a doctor she became a woman and said with considerable feelings, "Perhaps she was selling herself to bring milk for the baby. That is why he identifies himself both with the elder lost child and also with the baby lying on the footpath. He sees himself in every motherless child. That is why he throws stones at every pimp, who he thinks, is selling his mother."

The journalist asked the psychiatrist, "There must be some cure for this poor man. Otherwise he will go completely mad, he might even commit a murder."

"The cure for him is to be helped and educated to identify the forces that were responsible for the famine and for the death of his mother. His complex will go when he realises that he himself is the victim of the same forces which caused his mother's death. The death has to be avenged!"

From a doctor, now she was talking like a revolutionary. Then again she became a woman, the universal mother.

"Tell me, child, from which village did your parents come to Calcutta?"

From his semi-somnolence Amar Kaal momentarily came out, as he replied.

"From Naxalbari!"

"Naxalbari?" The psychiatrist repeated.

"We have never heard the name of this village," said Ajoy Bose, "maybe it is in Darjeeling district."

"I have been sleeping in a grave in Calcutta," replied Amar Kaal, still not out of his daze, "But I want to go to Naxalbari, Ma!"

"Look he is now taking you also for his mother," said Ajoy Bose.

"Ma!" Amar Kaal, suddenly coming out of his somnolence, said, "I will surely go to Naxalbari!"

The narrow gauge train was taking them–Ajoy Bose and Amar Kaal–to Naxalbari.

Across green jungles, hills, tea-plantations, paddy-fields—a vast expanse of green—the sight of which brought a smile to Amar Kaal's face. Now he was dressed in a dhoti and his red *banian* had been replaced by a shirt that was also dyed a vivid red, till, at last, the sign-board of NAXALBARI station came zooming out of the countryside.

Together, they got down from the train at the little station.

Ajoy Bose who had discarded his smart outfit, was now dressed in *khadi* kurta-pyjama, still carried his camera with him, and had a *jhola* slung over his shoulder.

They came out of the station by walking across the railway lines, and were soon in the village.

At the Chowringhee Sweet Shop which, they were told, was the meeting place of the revolutionaries, Ajoy Bose enquired, "Where are the forces of the revolution?"

The sweet-shop owner pointed to a footpath going out of the village. "They are there today."

2

RED FLOWERS BLOOM IN GREEN FIELDS

Walking along a *bund* in the fields, they came upon lush paddy crop. But, Amar Kaal wondered, were they paddy fields? From all he had heard, paddies didn't have red flowers. And here the fields were blooming with red flowers. Red against green! They looked very pretty. The smile was an unfamiliar phenomenon on his face!

"Red flowers, *Babuji*!" exclaimed Amar Kaal, smiling broadly.

"These are not red flowers but red flags," explained Ajoy Bose, "that the peasants have planted to assert their rights on these fields." Besides little red paper flags that looked like flowers, now Amar Kaal also saw big red flags to mark the boundaries of the fields.

As they walked through the red-flagged fields, some strange music was welling up in Amar Kaal's heart and soul. He had a sense of homecoming.

The journalist was now saying, "Comrade, this is your land. And, beyond that, maybe that is your village from where the jotedar and the sahukar had turned out your father and mother and driven them to their death on the Calcutta pavements."

The beautiful music of homecoming that Amar Kaal was hearing was now transformed into martial strains of a revolutionary music. This land, this village, was *his*—but he would have to fight for them! His fist and teeth were both clenched.

As they neared an oddly shaped tree, a sudden, sharp voice assailed their ears.

"*Kothay jaechhay*?"

They were momentarily taken aback by the unexpected question. "Where are you going?", but the journalist replied with a clenched fist.

"*Lal Salam. Amra tomar bandhoo* (We are your friends)."

A peasant boy, with a sharp sickle in his hand, jumped down from the tree and now confronted them.

"*Lal Salam.* Where are you coming from?"

Ajoy Bose informed the young guard. "We are coming from Calcutta. I am a reporter there. I have come to tell the world about the revolution here. This is my friend who has lived in a Calcutta graveyard. But as a child, during the great famine, he had gone with his parents from Naxalbari itself. Tell us about the revolution! How far has it progressed?"

The little boy pulled himself to his maximum height, as he proudly said, "All the surrounding villages have been liberated. The jotedar of the next village has been arrested. Tonight he will be put before the people's court."

And that brought a grim satisfaction to Amar Kaal, but also in his eyes was the cold fire of vengeance.

A torch was blazing...

Torches were balzing like the aroused anger of the peasants. The village square was festooned with red flags, with red banners, with portraits of Mao and Che, with revolutionary slogans. The jotedar was brought, bound with ropes and chains.

He was still clad in white dhoti and silk shirt, with gold buttons, studded with diamonds. An embroidered pashmina shawl lay across his shoulders. He held the folds of his starched dhoti in his manacled left hand.

"Comrades," thundered the judge, Comrade Dada, from his chair in the middle of the square, and the chatter of the multitude dissolved into the hush of expectancy as the armed peasants including Amar Kaal–armed with guns, with spears, with bows and arrows, or only with lathis.

Pointing to the jotedar who was short of stature but arrogant and defiant even in adversity, Comrade Dada continued, "Look well at this jotedar–Lalit Kumar Chowdhury–your class enemy, and your exploiter! All his life he has exploited you, beaten you, starved you, jailed you, and tortured you. Today, thanks to the revolution (cries of *Inqilab Zindabad!*), he has been brought before this people's court as a prisoner to receive the verdict of the "people". So let any of you bring the specific charges against him so that the jurors may get an idea of the enormity of his crimes."

Silence fell over the assembly as each thought back to recall all the crimes of the jotedar.

At last one old peasant got up. "My name is Appu, son of Ruldoo. One day, ten years ago, I happened to shit in the fields–because there was no latrine in the whole village. When he saw me doing this, he ordered his *lathials* to put it into my mouth. And they did as they were told. I demand the same thing be done to him today."

"Then there will be no difference between him and us, between the jotedar's justice and the people's justice!" said the judge, "But, Appu, we have duly noted your complaint. Any others?"

Another old peasant got up and said, "Comrades, this jotedar, this bastard..." He almost broke down before he could bring himself to utter the words, "...blackened his face with my daughter, and she committed suicide by drowning in the well."

There was a big commotion at this, cries of "Shame! Shame!" were heard, and one young man shouted, "Let his daughter be raped before his eyes."

The daughter of the jotedar, watching it all from the balcony of the jotedar's palace, cowered among the grim-faced womenfolk.

Comrade Dada silenced the agitated crowd and then, with a serious expression, asked, "Any volunteers?"

Several young and hefty peasants raised their hands–among them was also Amar Kaal.

"Fine revolutionaries you are!" Comrade Dada's voice had the ring of irony. "Always ready to rape the class enemy's daughter! But that is not revolutionary justice. Shame on you!"

Amar Kaal, shamed by Dada's words, put down his hand, followed by the others.

The court continued with its work.

One peasant was saying, "Once when the harvest was ruined by drought and I could not pay his rent and the interest on it, he ordered that my hands be put under the feet of his cot, and he and his men sat on it for one full hour till I fainted. Look, the bones of my hand and still broken..." He showed his broken hands to the assemblage.

There was much concern among the peasants, and much anger till another peasant rose to his feet. "Now I bring the most serious charge against the Jotedar." When the court and the peasants were all attention to him he said, "He had my brother,

Mithoo, a landless labourer beaten and tortured to death. His only fault was that he dared to answer him back when the Jotedar abused him. I demand the death penalty for that!"

Mithoo and his brother were Harijans, so while the Harijans raised their voices to support his demand for the death penalty, the crowd of caste peasants chose to remain silent.

Comrade Dada did not miss a thing in the behavior of the crowd.

"Mithoo was an untouchable–wasn't he? So he deserved to die. Don't you think so, comrades?"

Nobody dared reply to his question.

Amar Kaal had raised his hand. So Comrade Dada turned to him, "Yes, comrade! But I haven't seen you before?"

Amar Kaal, having caught the judge's eye, now rose to his feet. "It is true," he said, "that Comrade Dada has not seen me before. Nor has anyone else here. That is exactly my charge against the Jotedar. Thirty years ago, when he was a young man, he forced my parents and other peasants to leave the village, they had to walk all the way to Calcutta, my father who was already a sick man, died on the way, and I was born to take his place. My mother named me Amar Kaal so I should never forget the years of the great famine."

Tears were now coming into his eyes and his voice. "My mother had to sell her honour to buy milk for me...then she died or was taken away somewhere by someone of the city brothers of the Jotedar. And I had to live in a grave–for a poor man a grave is the safest place in that city of stones. But now thanks to that friend over there," and he pointed to Ajoy Bose, who was scribbling in his notebook, "I am back here, in the village where my father and mother were born and I demand that justice be meted out to the Jotedar." Then he sat down, relieved. He had done his duty. He had told his story and he was relieved of the tension.

"All right, comrade. All the crimes of the Jotedar are before the people's court. But, true to the concept of the "people's justice", we will give the accused a chance to defend himself–if he can! Speak up, Chowdhury, if you have something to say."

The jotedar was still unbroken, unbowed. He said arrogantly, "This is not a proper court, and I don't have to say anything before it. Soon..."

Just at this moment the boy whom Amar Kaal and the journalist had seen on a tree came running. "Comrade Dada, the police are coming in many jeeps and trucks."

Suddenly there was pandemonium and panic.

"No panic," said the judge, who was now commander-in-chief. "Take the prisoner to the lock-up in his room. And take your battle positions as you have been instructed. We shall die rather than give up the gains of our revolution."

"*Inqilab*–" he shouted.

"*Zindabad*!" Came the chorus.

"Death to the class enemy," came another chorus.

After the jotedar was taken away by two Red Guards, Comrade Dada came down from the dais and went to Ajoy Bose. "Comrade, you had better escape in the darkness."

When the journalist protested, saying, "I don't want to escape like a coward," the leader of the party explained to him, "No, comrade, it is important that there should be someone alive to tell the world what happened here. Maybe for a day or two, but there was a revolution here. Tell the people *that*. Goodbye."

"I hate to leave you, Comrade Dada!" said Ajoy Bose.

"I know. But you have to do it in the interest of the revolution. I order you to do that."

And so the journalist withdrew and handed back his gun to Amar Kaal. "Will you come with me?" he asked.

"No, comrade. I will stay and fight. I have lived all my life in a grave. If I die, it won't be any different. Goodbye. And thanks!" he ran to join the others who were hurriedly preparing a barricade.

But other peasants tried to persuade Comrade Dada to leave. "Your life is important for the revolution," they said. "So long as you are alive, the revolution will live."

"No, I will stay to fight with you. If I die, a dozen comrades will be here to take my place. Moreover, who is the commander here–you or me?

"The people have taken charge of the revolution–now we are the masters–and we are ordering you to go to Calcutta and keep the movement–and the name of Naxalbari–alive," said one of the peasants.

"Go, Comrade Dada, go–before we are rude to you!"

At last Comrade Dada reluctantly agreed to go along with the journalist who was waiting for him.

"I didn't want to go," said Comrade Dada, "What will the people say?"

The journalist had the last word, as they disappeared into the jungle. "They will say, 'It is hard to die for the *revolution*. But harder still is to *live* for the revolution.'"

There was silence everywhere. Silence and darkness. The torches had been extinguished.

The silhouettes of the police were seen across the barricades.

"Hold my place. I have an old debt to pay," said Amar Kaal to the peasant next to him in the barricades. "I will be back in a minute."

Amar Kaal ran towards the jotedar's house which was a massive silhouette in the distance. A police bullet fired at the fleeing shadow, just missed him, and was embedded in the wall just as he slipped in with his gun.

"Fire!" ordered the peasant-commander as the silhouettes of the police vehicles advanced towards the barricades.

A volley of fire and a flight of arrows ineffectively ricocheted from the armour-plated vehicles which continued to advance.

From the cover of the vehicles came a hail of machine-gun fire and several bombs which burst on the barricades. The police had brought the army for support.

They kept on raining death till the revolutionary peasants were decimated–all except one.

This was Amar Kaal who stood, gun at the shoulder, aimed at the jotedar.

His left eye squinted as he aimed through the sites of the gun.

There was the pent-up anger of thirty years of deprivation on his face–anger and hatred and fury.

Before his eye rose the image of his mother and himself as a child, of the pimp who had sold his mother–all conjured out of the *Dharti Ke Lal* shadows with which his own life was identified!

Soon the image of the jotedar was blurred by the tears that were flowing out of his eyes.

He pressed the trigger–once–twice–

But he did not hear the shot–nor the shouts of the jotedar in his death agony.

There was a deafening roar of the bombs as they fell on the revolutionary peasants' army, and that smothered Amar Kaal's violence and murder of the jotedar.

He wiped away his tears. Now a strange peace seemed to have come to him. He was not only avenged, he was cleansed.

He ran back to the lifeless barricades, didn't know what had happened.

"I killed the Jotedar," he confided to his neighbor, but when he didn't answer, he shook his shoulder. The severed arm came into his hand.

Meanwhile, the army was marching over the dead men of the barricades–they did not know that among the dead, there was a living one too–Amar Kaal, the man who had spent a lifetime in a grave, for whom Death was a friend and a comrade!

3

BOMBS FOR A TEA PARTY

The dead body of Surendranath Chakravarty was lying in his house. There was peace on his face. The voice of the DIG, booming over the loudspeaker in the jungle, came: "Surendranath Chakravarty!"

A hand rose in the air. It had a hammer and stickle tattooed on the arm. It was followed by 6 feet 3 inches of Surendranath Chakravarty.

The dead body of Anand Kumar Gangooly was lying in a pool of blood, his face smashed by a point-blank shot. The voice of the professor came: "Anand Kumar Gangooly."

A handsome and clean-looking youth got up and answered, "Yes, Sir."

The dead face of Anwarul Haq lying at the barricades. The voice of the DIG: "Anwarul Haq!"

The bearded Anwarul Haq got up to his feet and answered: "Yes, Sir."

The rest of the roll call followed.

Then the professor closed the muster roll with a bang and turned to the big blackboard on which Naxalite drawings and slogans were made with coloured chalk.

"Who did this? Stand up–if you have any courage!" thundered the professor with considerable anger and contempt in his voice.

Thereupon the tall figure of Chakravarty stood up.

"Hoon! So it is this *lamboo...*" thought the professor, but his thought was interrupted by three other boys and one slim girl also standing up.

"Anwarul Haq," said a short bearded fellow.

"Pradeep Sinha," announced a clean-shaven, smooth-cheeked youth.

"Inder Das Gupta," introduced a young Bengali with a little growth of beard.

"Kamala Sen," said the pretty girl.

The professor thought Naxalism must be a very contagious disease if the daughter of a Congress leader had also caught it.

"Get out, all of you!" commanded the professor and added, "You will be reported to the Principal and rusticated. Your educational career is at an end."

The five students, led by Chakravarty, trooped out, proud and erect–with no feeling of shame or remorse.

The professor turned to the handsome boy in the front row. "Anand Kumar Gangooly! You are not one of these hooligans! You stood first in the last terminal exam. And, I hope, you will do equally well in the annual examination. Now take out your copy of Hamlet and read out the soliloquy."

Anand Kumar Gangooly who had been in two minds whether or not to follow in the footsteps of his friends, now opened his copy of Hamlet and started reading out the soliloquy of the Prince of Denmark which revealed his own dilemma:

"*To be or not to be...*" And he looked out of the corner of his eye at the corridor below where his five friends were walking out of the college.

"*That is the question!*" And he chewed each word as if this was the crucial decision of his life!

Meanwhile, the five students were marching through the college corridor.

"It was done by me," said Surendranath Chakravarty, "Why did you all stand up and get explelled for nothing?"

Kamala Sen replied, "Because, comrade, you had written and drawn what was in our own minds and hearts."

"Kamala is right," assented Anwarul Haq.

"To hell with bourgeois education!" said Inder.

"Come on, then, let's go to Comrade Dada," suggested Pradeep Sinha, and all enthusiastically agreed.

They were walking out of the central gate of the college that they were waylaid by a young man, slightly older than they were, who was dressed in *khadi* silk slacks and bush shirt and had a camera slung over his shoulder.

"Is it true that you have been expelled for writing Maoist-Leninist slogans?" he asked them and they wondered who he was, and how the news had got to him so quickly.

"I am a journalist and it's my business to know these things," he explained, "My name is Ajoy Bose. I suppose you want to meet Comrade Dada. Come, I will tell you where you may find him."

The human skull was grinning at the comedy-tragedy of life which had brought him, a homeless beggar, into the house of a medical student.

Also grinning was the impish Ajitha, the kid sister of Surendranath Chakravarty who was trying to write an article sitting at his desk in a lower-middle-class house in South Calcutta.

"*Ki kor chis* (What are you doing, grinning away like this)?" asked the disturbed brother.

"I am just looking at this skull and wondering why it is grinning" replied the first-year medical student, Ajitha.

"All you medical students are crazy," taunted her brother, then added more seriously, "You should know that there is nothing in this skull–whatever wisdom lies is in the human brain."

Ajitha replied back, "Like the wisdom that is in your brain?" She tapped her brother's crown with her hand and was gone inside to her mother in the kitchen.

Surendranath once again tried to concentrate on his article when he heard his name being shouted.

"Surendra-*da*! Surendra-*da*!" came the voice of Anand.

"*Aray*, Anand, *ki khobar*?" he greeted his young friend in Bengali, then added, "*Aao, Aao.*"

He brought him from the door and made him sit down on the divan-cum-bed, the most comfortable place in that sparsely furnished room. "*Bosh, bosh* (Sit down, sit down)..."

Then he called his sister in a loud enough voice to be heard in the kitchen. "Ajitha! Ajitha!"

"*Ki bolchis, Dada* (What is it, elder brother)?" came her reply and she followed her voice.

"You know Anand, don't you?" said her brother, as she coyly namaskared his friend. He namaskared her back.

"Bring some tea for him, will you?" Surendranath ordered his sister, casually.

She ran into the kitchen, humming a love-lyric of Tagore. It was apparent that she was excited about this unexpected arrival of Anand, who was more than just her brother's friend. In her happy excitement, she touched the boiling kettle and burnt her dainty fingers. She had to put them into her mouth and suck them.

Meanwhile, Anand was saying to Chakravarty, "Forgive me, Surendra-*da*."

"What is there to forgive?" asked his taller—and older—friend.

"I didn't leave the class with all of you! I was in two minds. Like Hamlet. *To be or not to be?* Perhaps I am also a coward!"

"*Nahin, yaar,*" Chakravarty casually dismissed his doubts, "I know you are not a coward. The whole trouble is that you are still not convinced about our policy and programme. When you are convinced, you will surely join us. Till that time..." He wanted to say more but he saw his sister entering with tea and snacks, and left the sentence unfinished. "There—your tea has come."

Ajitha offered the cup of tea and a plate containing *luchi-tarkari* to Anand who accepted the tea, but questioned about the snacks. "What's this?" meaning thereby, "What is the need of all this?"

Ajitha replied literally to the question, "It is *luchi-tarkari*! That's all!"

"Thanks," mumbled Anand, self-conscious in the presence of her brother.

"You finish your tea and I will change in the meantime. I have to go out somewhere," said Chakravarty and he disappeared behind the curtains.

After he was gone, Anand turned to Ajitha. "What was the occasion for all this?" he said, pointing to the *luchi-tarkari*.

"You are coming straight from the college. Must be feeling hungry! And does one offer a plain cup of tea without any snacks?"

Anand gallantly remarked, looking at her intently, "Hunger disappears the moment I look at you!" Then he added in Bengali, "*Tomkay dekhay amar shob kichu bhool hoye jae.*" Quoting a dialogue from some Bengali play he had seen.

Ajitha briefly, and coyly, answered in one word, "*Satti* (Is that true)?"

Just then her brother came out, dressed to go out in *khaddar* kurta-pyjama with a cloth *jhola* over his shoulder.

"What happened?" he asked both of them.

"Look, Dada," she replied quickly, "He does not want to eat anything."

"*Aray*, eat something with your tea! By the way, I am going out."

"Where are you going?" Anand innocently asked.

"On some important work!" replied Chakravarty, without elaborating any further.

"I'll also come with you!" offered Anand, getting up.

"I can't tell you where. Nor can I take you with me." Then he called out, "Ma! Ma!"

The mother came out, adjusting the *pallu* of her white widow's sari over her head.

"You know, Mother, this is my best friend, Anand."

"Yes, yes, I now him quite well." She turned round to her son's friend who was bending low to touch her feet. "May you live long, son." Then she turned round to Surendranath, "What so special has happened today?"

"Ma! I'm going out on an important job. If anything should happen to me, Anand will look after you both."

"What are you saying, son? God bless you! Why should something happen to you? You are talking like your father talked before he went to war."

"Yes, Mother, this is also WAR–but quite different from father's war."

And he cast a fleeting look at the portrait of his deceased father–in an army captain's uniform.

He quickly touched his mother's feet and gently caressed the hand of his sister, then he patted the shoulder of Anand and went out.

The mother had a sense of foreboding. Her son was all the time coming and going, but never before had he observed rituals of such an elaborate leave-taking.

"Ajitha, do you know where he is going?"

"No, Mother," replied the daughter, telling the truth, but not the whole truth, for she had an inkling about where he was going.

The mother quickly went out into the verandah, looked out through the bamboo-curtain, saw her son—how tall he was, just like his father—striding away.

"*Khoka*," she called out, as she had called him in childhood. For her he would always be a child.

Then she remembered what her mother used to say. "When a man of the house goes out, never call out after him. It might bring him bad luck!"

So she put her hand to her mouth to stifle herself.

Ajitha was asking Anand, "Do you know where Dada has gone?"

"I don't know exactly," he replied, "but I have a hunch where he is headed. I wish I too could go with him—on the same path!"

And little Ajitha, a first-year medical student, and freshly in love, suddenly felt grown up, as she mumbled, "It is the path that I too want to tread."

The dead face of Comrade Dada was in the circle of light.

The same face, now alive, giving himself an insulin injection, reacts to the sound of someone knocking on the door.

"*Kay, kay ukhanay* (Who is there)?" He asks in Bengali.

"*Lal Salam*, Comrade Dada," came Chakravarty's reply from outside.

Then the old man turned to one of his assistants to open the door but with a gesture of his hand.

The five students entered the hut-like cottage which was decorated with big Naxalite posters and with large portraits of Mao, Marx, Lenin and Che Guevara. They looked around them and were duly impressed by the revolutionary atmosphere.

"*Ki baypar*?" asked Comrade Dada, "What do you want?"

Chakravarty replied on behalf of the whole group. "Till this morning, we were all students of the Presidency College. Now we want to join your party!"

"Is this a tea party that you can gatecrash uninvited?" Comrade Dada's words were full of sarcasm.

"We know, it is not a tea party but a political party," replied Chakravarty.

"If you want to join a political party," Comrade Dada was still sarcastic, "then join the Congress. If you don't like the Congress, there are two socialist parties for you–these two communist parties also." It was evident that his sarcasm was aimed at them specially. "Join one of them if you like. There are other political parties also. There is the Bharatiya Jana Sangh. There is the Swatantra Party."

Kamala Sen, who had kept a decorous silence so far, now spoke up. "But, Dada, we want to join the Marxist-Leninist Party."

"Then give me one good reason why you want to join this party?" asked Comrade Dada, now in a more business-like manner.

Chakravarty had the answer pat on his tongue. "Because we are anxious to quicken the pace of revolution, and that we know only your party can accomplish!"

Comrade Dada was still not sure of their bonafides, so he asked, "Who sent you here? The police–isn't that so?"

The bearded Inder now spoke with a sense of injured pride, "Shall we have to prove our bonafides?"

"Yes," agreed Comrade Dada, "no one knows this address. The police can give you a big reward for revealing the whereabouts of our party headquarters. Tell me who revealed this address to you?"

Pradeep Sinha, the Bihari, now spoke, "It was Comrade Ajoy Bose who directed us here! I think he is one of your trusted fellows."

"That's all right," assented Comrade Dada, "But what will your families say?" Sharply turning to the tall young man, he asked, "What does your father do?"

Chakravarty replied without any hesitation, "My father is dead. My mother is a school teacher."

Dada turned to the bearded Muslim, "What does your father do?"

"He is a hosiery merchant," answered Anwarul Haq.

Now Dada turned to Kamala Sen, "And who is your father?"

"My—my—my father—" Kamala was clearly hesitant to reveal her father's identity. "My father is the Congress leader, Mukul Sen."

"*Achchha!*" Comrade Dada was quite surprised to hear the name of his old friend and now political enemy—but he did not reveal all he knew about the Congress leader whom he still remembered as Motu Muku. "So you are Mukul Babu's daughter. That is why you are wearing such an expensive *khaddar* sari. But wearing a red silk blouse won't bring revolution quicker."

Kamala Sen was equal to the challenge, "*Ji*," she replied, "I will completely change myself. I can do anything for revolution."

Now it was the turn of the lean and hungry-looking Inder Das Gupta.

"My father is a doctor."

Pradeep Sinha, the Bihari, was the last to be interrogated about his father's identity.

"My father is a lawyer in Patna!" he said in answer to Comrade Dada's question.

"*Achchha!*" With a nod Comrade Dada enrolled them all in the army of the revolution. "For some days you will have to do postering on the walls of the city–" indicating towards the slogans on the posters. "This work will be a test of your wits and your revolutionary zeal because the police is after our boys. Anyone found postering in the city is liable to be shot. If you survive, you will be sent to work in the villages of Bengal or Bihar. Among the landless and the tribals. That is the real seat of revolution. And there your work will be no less full of hazards. Do you accept this bargain of death?"

All replied in chorus, "Yes, Comrade Dada. We accept this bargain!"

"Have you got some arms?" questioned the wily Comrade Dada with a disarming casualness.

They looked at each other. Then Chakravarty, taking out a fat book from his *jhola*, said, "Our weapons are these books."

And he handed over that volume to the leader, like a vassal presenting tribute to a king.

Dada took the book in his hand, mentally weighed it, then pronounced, "It contains a pistol!" And when he uncovered the binding of the book, inside it was, indeed, a revolver in the hollowed-out pages.

Inder too, presented a book to Dada who, likewise, weighed it in his hand and said, 'There is one hand grenade in it."

Sure enough, when he opened it, there was a round, wire-bound hand bomb in it.

"Keep these toys over there," ordered Comrade Dada pointing to the top of a shelf.

4

REVOLVER AND RABINDRA SANGEET

A service revolver in a holster was placed on a table as Mr Gangooly, the deputy inspector general, divested himself of his uniform.

There was a portrait of Tagore on the wall glowering down on the police uniform.

From the bathroom came the sound of a shower, then the humming of a Tagore song as Mr Gangooly scrubbed himself.

Then the bathroom door opened, and Mr Gangooly—not the DIG—emerged dressed in a muslin kurta and dhoti—an immaculate *bhadralok*.

Mrs Gangooly—a handsome 40-year-old—entered, dressed like an upper-class Bengali housewife, with a gold necklace, and a bunch of keys tied to the sari end.

"*Shoon cho*. Are you bathed and changed? Shall I get you some tea?"

"No Sumitra. I had tea in the office. Just get my sitar. I want to practise some Rabindra Sangeet before dinner."

She went to a corner, and brought a sitar from its covering, and handed it over to her husband who was by now enthroned on the velvet-covered divan. He accepted the sitar with due reverence, and bowed before the portrait of Gurudev who continued to glower down on the police officer-cum-Rabindra-Sangeet fan.

Mr Gangooly closed his eyes and touched the strings of the sitar with the *mizrab*. A lilting Tagore melody poured out from the sitar.

Mrs Gangooly sat down in a corner, enjoying her husband's playing, but Tagore was not pleased. It was obvious from the expression of the portrait that the bearded old man was not very happy with this *chela* of his.

During the music, Anand–whom we had already seen in the college and in the house of his friend Chakravarty, looked in through the open door. He was obviously returning from the college, with one or two books in his hand, and namaskared to his father and mother.

The father, loathed to interrupt his musical session–for it soothed his nerves after his duty in the police station, just silently nodded in the direction of his son, acknowledging the son's greeting with a smile. The mother, however, blessed the son with a prayer for his long life, then told him to go and have a bath as the dinner would be soon ready.

Mr Gangooly was in the full regalia of his uniform–but only in his portrait on the wall of the dining room.

The dining table was loaded with food–there was fish curry, fried fish, Delhi rice, peas pulao, curd, vegetables of several kinds, chapatties and *parathas*.

There were only four people to eat all this–Mr and Mrs Gangooly, their son Anand, and their little daughter Anamika. Mr Gangooly occupied the head of the table with his wife at the other end, his son and daughter occupying the chairs to his left and right.

The indulgent mother was pursuing her son to take one more *paratha*. "Come on, Anand, you are eating very little today. Have one more *paratha* with this fish curry. I have specially prepared it for you, for it is your favourite."

"Mother, you are asking me to have a third *paratha*, while millions in this country are not getting even one dry chapatti a day!"

"What's that?" Mr Gangooly immediately reacted, "That sounds like Naxalite talk to me! Have you also been infected with this dangerous ideology?"

"I was only mentioning these *parathas* dripping with ghee," replied his son, "while millions are starving in the country."

"Don't forget," taunted his father, "that all your blood and bones are built out of the same ghee and flour that goes into these *parathas*."

Anand did not give any reply, only silently nibbled at the food.

His mother tried to change the topic. "Tell me, Anand, how are you getting on with your studies?"

"I am doing quite well. Only yesterday my English professor was hoping that I will stand first in the annual examination. He liked my rendering of the soliloquy of Hamlet very much."

"What soliloquy?" chimed in his sister.

"You won't understand. *To be or not to be?*"

"You tell me one thing," his father butted in, "Are there any Naxalites in your college or not? Our last intelligence report says there is much Naxalite talk heard in and around the Presidency College."

"Yes, I guess so," replied Anand but without emphasis.

"Have they tried to brainwash you and seek your help in their nefarious, murderous activities?" Mr Gangooly asked, now seriously transformed into the deputy inspector general. And his son, the diffident student, replied, "No"–and that was the truth!

No one had tried to brainwash him, but his brain was itself infected! But *that* his father had not asked him.

"Well you keep away from them–do you hear?" His father finally warned him.

And Anand said, "Yes, Baba."

The dinner was now over. Mr Gangooly went into the bathroom, while the servant began to clear the table. Little Anamika retired to her room. Only the mother and Anand remained, still seated on their respective chairs.

Mrs Gangooly said, her handsome face clouded over with an unknown anxiety, "What is the matter with you, Anand? You appear to have something on your mind?"

Anand tried to change his expression, even forced a smile. "No, Ma, it's nothing!"

"Were you offended by anything your father said?" the mother persisted.

"No, Ma," the son replied, "Nothing that my father says can offend me anymore."

On his mother's face was a pall of anxiety.

Somewhere in North Calcutta...

Five young Naxalites were doing what in the common parlance of their party was called "postering".

Over a boundary wall was poured down whitener.

Over it appeared in big red lettering:

INQILAB ZINDABAD-NAXALBARI LAL SALAM!

Posters with portraits of revolutionary leaders like Mao and Che Guevara were pasted nearby. All this was done quickly at extra fast speed—within minutes of the "postering", the five had to make the getaway.

But one of them delayed the process with her question.

Under the portrait of Mao Tse-tung, while a lettering poster was up reading, "The Chairman of China is our Chairman", Kamala Sen, now considerably deglamourised, but still looking beautiful in her red-bordered white sari pulled up like a working woman, asked a passing comrade of hers, while looking at the forceful out-thrust jaw of Mao: "Can't great leaders like Mao Tse-tung be born in India too?"

Inder to whom the question was addressed replied, "Yes, they can be—but this poster represents the party policy which cannot be questioned." Then, he looked left and right, to make sure this doubting question and its equally dangerous reply had not been overheard by any of their comrades. The Naxalite young men, who were proving a terror, were themselves in terror of their leaders and of each other!

Suddenly a boy who was keeping watch upon the wall blew a warning whistle and there was panic among the Naxalites. The police were coming! Tall Chakravarty who was the leader of this group, stood near the wall, with his hands joined to make an improvised step to help four of his comrades to get away. One after the other, they—including Kamala Sen—were helped to climb over to safety. There was a reassuring sound of scurrying feet. But the policemen, *dandas* in hand, were already approaching him before he could be sure of his own safety. Two of his comrades hiding in a corner, pounced on the pair of policemen, and knocked them unconscious. Chakravarty helped them also to climb to safety. Then as he was about to climb the wall himself, three other policemen surrounded him. But he, the tall one, was a match for all of them. He slipped through the grip of one of them, and gave fist blows to two of them. His karate training came to his help. Then he started scrambling over the wall when he was taken unawares by the third policeman. Chakravarty gave him a hard kick–something he had learnt in his karate club–and sent him sprawling backwards. Then as he climbed the wall, he saw the policemen on the other side of the wall.

He ran over the wall just as dawn was breaking over Calcutta, he could see the swimming pool of College Square in the distance. He ran on and on to avoid the police who were chasing him below the wall–till he came to the part of the wall just under some high-rise buildings. And now he saw two policemen coming towards him on top of the wall. So he turned back. Meanwhile, two of his pursuers had also climbed the wall behind him. He was trapped from both sides. He stood on the spot, his tall frame dwarfed by the still taller buildings. The police parties were approaching him from both sides. But still they were cautious, holding their *dandas* at the ready. Chakravarty, realising that that was the end, whipped out a knife from his *jhola*–he was sorry Dada had not allowed them to have any bombs or grenades on them, or he would have destroyed the whole pursuing police force. Still he had the knife with him and he knew how to wield it. He would kill one or two before he could be killed–or captured!

But the revolver of a police inspector, standing on the rough ground below the wall, was already aimed at him. Before the Naxalite's knife could do any damage, the bullet had been fired and suddenly there was excruciating pain in the pit of Chakravarty's stomach where the bullet had drilled a hole.

The open clasp knife fell from his hand and came clattering down on the stones below. His hand went up involuntarily to press where he had been hit and the whole world was reeling, revolving. The sky-scraper was tumbling down and the earth was coming up to embrace it.

The next moment Chakravarty was sprawled on the ground below. He never knew where and when he fell, or what happened afterwards.

The Inspector ordered his men to "phone to the police station to send an ambulance." "We have at least caught one of them, but he must be rushed to the hospital at once, or he won't be able to tell us the address of the Naxalite hideouts in the city."

Soon the clanking bell of the ambulance could be heard in the distance, coming nearer...

5

WE ARE ALSO REVOLUTIONARIES!

A young college girl was crying by the roadside where Chakravarty and another Naxalite found her in their locality.

"What happened, sister?" asked the tall young man.

The girl obviously did not know him to be Naxalite, for she said, "These Naxalites are again at it. Last week they kidnapped the son of a neighbor of ours, and demanded–and got–a ransom of a thousand rupees. This time they say they need money again for their revolution, and they have snatched away my gold chain and my gold bangles. 'Don't worry,' they say, 'it's all for the revolution.'"

"Are you sure they said they were Naxalites?" asked Mohan, who was a new recruit to the party.

"Yes, Dada, they are Naxalites all right!"

"Where have they gone?" Chakravarty asked a more direct and practical question. Already a plan was being formed in his mind.

"That way, Dada," said the girl pointing to a lane.

"Come on, we'll give them a surprise visit," aaid Chakravarty to his comrade and dragged him into the lane.

"*Lal Salam*" came the password from the closed door and, on getting a clearance from Dada, one of the boys opened the door.

Three Naxalites entered, each dragging one other young man with him. Each of the three strangers had his hands tied at his back and his eyes blindfolded. One of them was a *pahelwan* type, one was a vicious-looking, short fellow, the third was also one obvious rogue.

"Whom have you brought?" demanded Comrade Dada.

"These are the *mastaans* of this locality who are giving us a bad name in the area," answered Chakravarty.

"What are they doing?" was Dada's next question.

"Blackmailing people–kidnapping their children–extorting money–all in the name of the Naxalites. They are using the front page of Naxalite pamphlets to write their warning notes. So the people take them to be Naxalites, and their activities as Naxalite activities" was the reply that one of the students gave him.

Comrade Dada signaled to his boys to remove the handkerchiefs with which the *mastaans* were blindfolded.

As they blinked their eyes, Comrade Dada shot his question–like a revolver bullet. "Is this true?"

The wrestler-type *mastaan* was equal to the challenge.

"Yes–and no," he replied, guardedly, "The facts are correct. The motives that are ascribed to us are untrue. Whatever we do, we do for the revolution."

"Is that so?" asked the leader, narrowing his eyes.

"We might be unknown to you," said the vicious-looking fellow among the *mastaans*, "but we are all revolutionaries. We have our party, policy and programme!"

Comrade Dada was looking at the portrait of Che Guevara on the wall by his side. "Do you follow the Che Guevara line, comrades?" asked the old man.

The *mastaans* had obviously never heard of Che Guevara. The *pehalwan*, obviously their ring-leader, replied, "What is Shay Goo-ve-ra? And what is this railway line of his?"

"I understand your difficulty," said Comrade Dada, "Few know this line which passes through hills and very difficult terrain to reach the end."

Then he signaled to his boys to retie the handkerchiefs on the eyes of the *mastaans*, saying "Now take them to their *proper* place"—with just a deep emphasis to the word "proper".

"I hope you don't mind," said one of the Naxalites while blindfolding his prisoners.

"That's all right," replied one of the *mastaans*, "These precautions are taken in any revolutionary party."

After they were blindfolded, Comrade Dada made the chopping gesture with his hand, which meant that they were dispensable and must be finished off.

"Don't push us, *sala*...I'll see you!" said the wrestler-*mastaan* as they were pushed out of the hut into the street.

"These are no Naxalites," said the vicious-looking *mastaan*, "They are just amateurs."

"We are the real Naxalites" boasted the third *mastaan*.

Out in the street, while passing a deserted corner, the hefty *mastaan* tried to wrest his hand free from the powerful grip of Chakravarty.

"Eh, *sala*, leave my hand—are we your prisoners?"

"No, my friend, that was all a show for our Comrade Dada," replied Chakravarty—but without letting the *mastaan* get free.

"*Achcha*! That means you are prepared to work with us?" asked the *mastaan*.

"Shshsh," warned one of the comrades of Chakravarty, "No such talk here."

"Then where shall we talk business?" asked one of the *mastaans* impatiently.

"Don't worry," reassured one of the Naxalites, "It will take place at our other hideout."

"Who else will be there?" suspiciously asked a *mastaan*.

"No one," assured Chakravarty, "You will be there–and we will be there–at least two of us. The third man we will leave out to keep watch, while we talk."

The Naxalites, pushing the *mastaans*, brought them to a disused garage which, sometime, they used as one of their hideouts.

Here they unbound the bandages from the eyes and hands of the *mastaans* and Chakravarty handed back the knife to the hefty *mastaan*.

The moment the clasp-knife was back in his hand, the *mastaan*'s original aggressive nature reasserted itself. Now he was the top-dog. His hands were at last free–and there was a clasp-knife in one of them. He will show these Naxalites a trick or two.

"That's right," he said, opening the knife with a click and holding it threateningly, "Now, suppose, I finish you off, what then?"

The next moment the powerful kick of Chakravarty got the *mastaan*'s hand with the knife and sent if flying away in the junk of the garage, while he took a karate stance.

The *mastaan* then realised that he had met his match in the tall Naxalite. He admired his adversary as a professional and turned to explain it as a practical joke, laughing it off.

"What will you get from us?" said Chakravarty, "our pockets are all empty."

"But not mine," said another Naxalite, "there is this revolver in it–and this revolver, too, is not empty." He took out the weapon and covered the *mastaans* with it. "There are also some bombs in there." He pointed to an empty crate in which half a dozen balls tied with rope were lying—presumably bombs.

"I was just joking," said the *peehaelwan-mastaan*, then digging into his pocket he brought out a wad of notes and throwing it up like a ball he said, "Have you ever seen so much money?"

"No, *yaar*," said Chakravarty, "we only risk our lives for revolution, so much money even our leader hasn't got."

"That old man is a mere bookworm," said one of the *mastaans*, "What nonsense was he talking?"

"But he has a great store of arms," said Mohan, the Naxalite, "four revolvers he has got beside this one here with me, and countless bombs."

"*Aray*, you are, indeed, our guru," said the vicious-looking *mastaan*, "Just go and get one or two revolvers and a dozen bombs. Then it will be fine!"

"That's right, *sala*," gleefully shouted the third *mastaan*, "With all these arms with us we can go for *big actions*—like a bank, for instance!"

The two Naxalites moved to go, and, while going, turned back to reassure the *mastaans*, "If we are delayed there, don't get upset. We will have to make sure the old man is asleep. Only then we can remove his arms."

After they were gone the three *mastaans* sat down on empty petrol-tins, having a hearty chuckle at the expense of the gullible Naxalites. "Haven't we fooled them nicely?" said one of them, "Let them bring the revolvers and the bombs and then we will show them what is what."

Chakravarty, the tall Naxalite, was telephoning from a public booth.

"Lal Bagh Police Station? This is to report big Naxalite activity around Mastaanbari in South Calcutta. Three of them with bombs are present in a garage in House No. 144, Lower Chatarpur Road. But they are armed with clasp-knives, revolvers and bombs. Be careful."

"Thank you," came the police officer's voice, "We will be there right away. But who are you?"

The Naxalite did not answer, just put back the receiver on its cradle.

"What's the news, Chakravarty?" asked Comrade Dada when the tall boy returned to the headquarters.

"I have telephoned to Lal Bagh Police Station."

"That we know. Then what happened?"

"Dada, I have seen everything with my own eyes!"

"What did you see?"

"I saw that the police caught them red-handed with half a dozen bombs. Also Naxalite posters were on the walls of the garage.

"Which you had planted there—isn't it?" interposed Comrade Dada. Chakravarty nodded.

"So the police didn't ask any questions, they started beating them mercilessly and dragged them away. The police officer was very happy at the big catch of three armed Naxalites. He is expecting a promotion!"

"Well done."

Sinha, who was grimly sitting in a corner, put in a divergent view. "We should not have informed the police. After all, they are all our enemies."

Dada weighed his words, then gave his verdict, "Both are our enemies—let the two mad dogs tear each other." Then, turning to Chakravarty, he said, "You did well to set them fighting against each other!"

6

A MINIATURE HELL

When he regained consciousness, his wound perfunctorily patched up, Chakravarty found himself strapped to a bench in a cell in the police station–the notorious and dreaded Lal Bazar Police Station.

The rays of the fading sunlight coming in through the grilled window were throwing shadows across his face. Otherwise the room was gloomy and dark. It is a small hell, Chakravarty mused from his lying position, as he surveyed the room.

As his senses revived, he could feel the pain in his abdomen where the bullet had hit him. The bullet itself had been removed but the gaping wound was still there, unattended. Septicaemia had already set in.

But he was conscious and able to talk.

That is what the police officers were concerned with.

An interrogation had already taken place, with one question that was repeated several times.

"Where are the Naxalite headquarters? Where is your leader, the one you call 'Comrade Dada'?"

But to every question Chakravarty had only one reply, "I don't know."

And when the question was put to him with more than normal insistence, he would defiantly answer, "I won't tell you."

Then the inspector had, for some reason, called off the interrogation. There was a few minutes respite to let the wounded prisoner recover some of his strength, or may be just to add to his torture of suspense.

So this was the moment he had rehearsed a hundred times in his mind. How would he stand up to torture? Would he die, rather than open his mouth? Or, would he speak like a rat?

He heard approaching heavy footsteps.

He saw, through the corner of his eye, the inspector followed by a havildar.

The inspector was smoking a cigar.

Just seeing him, Chakravarty (who had been a heavy smoker) had a hankering for a cigarette.

The inspector, standing over him, seemed to be a mind-reader. He turned to his havildar and said, "Give the poor man a cigarette."

The havildar took a cigarette out of his shirt pocket and inserted it between the prisoner's lips.

Then he struck a match and applied the little flame to the cigarette. Chakravarty pulled at the cigarette though it was not easy, for his lips were chapped and his throat was dry.

Still inhaling smoke helped to ease the tension of suspense. "What next?" he was thinking while inhaling the smoke and puffing out through his inert lips and nostrils.

Suddenly he saw the cigarette pulled out of his mouth. There was a cruel leer on the face of the havildar. The next moment he was snubbing the burning cigarette on the cheek of Chakravarty. The prisoner screamed aloud, as the smell of burning flesh rose in the air. But he was still a defiant "I can't, I won't". The cigarette was crushed against different portions of his cheek and lips, but after the first excruciating pain, it was less and less painful. Chakravarty thought to himself, "If that is all the torture, I think I can stand it." He grit his teeth so that when the cigarette was applied again, no sound came out from him.

The inspector, puffing at the cigar, felt defeated, cheated, by this doomed young man. What gave him such powers of resistance? Was it the accursed ideology of communism? He had dealt with other communists in his life, but these young men seemed to be made of a different, sterner, stuff! He would have to think of some new tortures to get something out of this tall young man, whose legs were longer than the longest bench that he could provide!

So he winked to the havildar who came up to him. The inspector whispered something in his ear.

The havildar silently nodded in agreement to what was proposed.

He took from a corner an extra-large scissor, the cross-blades of which gleamed in the blinding flashlight which was suddenly switched on. The strapped prisoner could only helplessly look on as the scissors were applied to cut his bandages. He screamed as the thin edge of the blade roughly scraped his raw wound.

"No, no," he screamed as he sensed what was coming. They were going to probe his wound with the scissors. He once again gritted his teeth as he waited for the torture to begin.

But his imagination could not reach the sadistic depravity to which his torturers would descend.

The havildar stood on a low stool on level with the bench and dug the wheel of his heavy boot directly into the open stomach wound, then systematically ground it with a circular movement of the heel.

It was the ultimate in pain.

It was pain beyond him, beyond endurance!

It was more painful than a meat-grinder put into the raw flesh of the wound. But it was more painful than any pain. It was continuous pain, in one continuing, unending current—like a mill stone which was grinding down his ideology, his resistance. Death would be infinitely preferable to this torture. He wished he could die and be relieved of this pain. He had never even dreamt in his worst nightmares, anything approaching this circular, grinding pain. At that moment, he felt, he could sell his party, his parents, his mother, sister and betray all his friends and comrades.

He screamed—and heard it, like someone else's blood-curdling scream!

"Yes, yes—I will tell you—I will tell you everything!"

It was only then that the heel was taken out of the wound, dripping with blood and pus, and Chakravarty finding, out of sheer exhaustion, relief! The flashlight was switched off.

Dawn was breaking over the eastern horizon but the street lamps were not yet extinguished.

In the half-light a car could be seen streaking along at a fast pace, past the Victoria Memorial.

A sleepy policeman, on patrol duty, where there were no automatic traffic signals, suddenly raised his arm and the car came to a screeching halt.

The policeman was apparently very rude and voluble as he lectured the errant motorist—who was none else than Ajoy Bose, the journalist. Then he wrote something in his notebook, tore off the leaf and gave it—presumably a notice to appear in court to answer charges of violation of traffic rules! The journalist glanced at the paper and then, bidding farewell to the grim-faced policeman, drove off.

The smoke from the earthenware *unun*—the charcoal-burning *angithees*—rising in the early morning air in the *bustee*.

Some of this smoke even entered the bamboo-matting walls of the hut where Comrade Dada was staying.

"*Ki khobar* (What is the news)?" asked the old man as the journalist entered.

Squatting down on the floor, near Dada, he whispered, "It is bad news, Dada. That college boy Chakravarty could not stand the torture and has told them the address of this place."

"How do you know?"

"From our usual source, Dada. The police are planning a raid on this place today. You must move to another place quickly."

And with that he took leave of his leader, for his utility to the party as a contact-man and a source of information, knowing he would be finished if he was arrested there along with the rest of them!

After he was gone, Dada turned to his boys.

"We have immediately to shift to some other place," he announced.

"We can then go to the other place."

"If the coward is squeezed about this place, he will give them the other address too. We have to find some absolutely unexpected place, at least for a few days."

Amar Kaal who was sprawled on a trunk in a corner sat up and said.

"I can accommodate all of them in my grave?"

"All of them?" exclaimed Dada. "And you will bury them in one grave?"

"No, I have a whole graveyard at my disposal," he elaborated his earlier statement.

Two havildars of the Calcutta Police, while perfunctorily *hunting* Naxalites, found a couple of Naxalite posters on the wall of the British cemetery in Park Circus.

This prompted them to look in and when they sauntered in, they saw a bearded fellow–obviously an artist but, maybe, a Naxalite bent over his sketching board.

"*Achchha!*" one of them remarked, "This is where they manufacture all the posters!"

The other agreed, "Yes, we will catch them red-handed."

So with their batons in hand, they advanced towards the artist who went on with his work.

When they were very near him, he ran with his sketching board, carefully hiding it from the view of the havildars.

It was a comical chase.

The artiste-Naxalite in front–the pot-bellied havildars in hot pursuit–zigzagging through the bushes and the undergrowth, running over the gravestones, stumbling over the open graves–

At last they caught the panting artist.

"Come on, out with it! Let us see your Naxalite poster. You know it is forbidden to make such things."

The artist reluctantly parted with his sketch board.

When the havildars saw it, it fell from their hands. It was so *hot*–a nude figure of a girl!

"*Aray*," they could hardly hide their shock of discovery, "this is *art*, we thought it was a subversive poster."

They gingerly handed back the sketch board to the bearded artist.

"Sorry, Saheb—we mistook you for a Naxalite."

Saying this they walked away and only after they had gone away, the other Naxalites emerged from their *graves* and shook hands with the bearded artist who removed the nude sketch and revealed, underneath, a Naxalite poster.

The door of the hut was kicked open by the booted inspector.

Followed by two policemen and one havildar, he entered what he expected to be the secret headquarters of the Naxalites, but he found it completely empty. No furniture, no books, no posters. But what were these discoloured oblongs on the walls?—Surely there had been posters here—Naxalite posters—so it was not entirely a false address that lanky Chakravarty had given. But obviously the Naxalites had been tipped off by somebody and they had got away to another place. Who could have tipped them off? Not Chakravarty—he was in no condition to warn anyone. Perhaps someone (he figured out with a grim expression), someone in the police station. Who? If only he knew the culprit's name.

Meanwhile they searched the empty hut and were ultimately rewarded with one empty capsule of INSULIN, the drug that was injected to patients of diabetes.

It was mentioned in the police records that the Naxalite leader, whom they called "Comrade Dada", was a chronic patient of the sugar disease.

NAYA SANSAR
MITHUN CHAKRABORTY
SMITA PATIL
THE NAXALITES
A FILM WITH A CONSCIENCE!
WRITTEN PRODUCED & DIRECTED BY
K.A. ABBAS
A

Film poster

Nana Palsikar as Dada Comrade

Mithun Chakravarty as Amar Kaaal

Dada Comrade Nana Palsikar, Sumit Mukherjee (Suren)

Priyadarshni as Kamala

Anand and the DIG from a scene in the film

The hideout of the Naxalites in the film

Dada Comrade, Suren and others

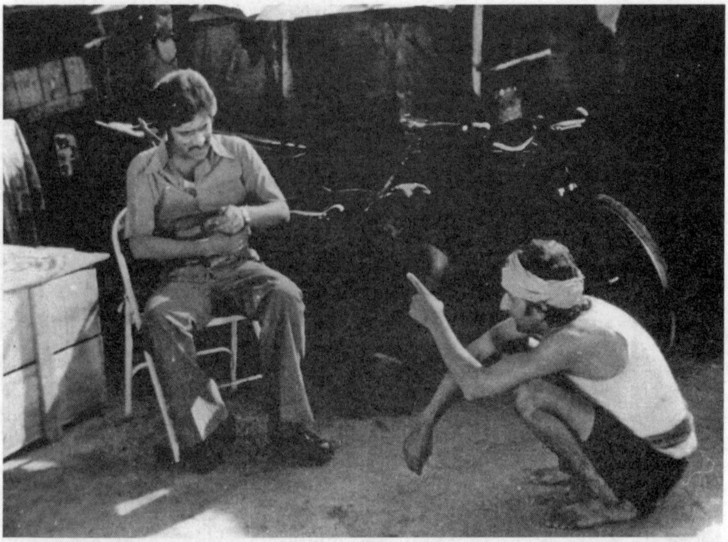

Tinnu Anand as Jaggu

Imtiaz Khan as revolutionary

Smita Patil as Ajitha in the prison

* *All photographs have been sourced from the National Film Archives of India*

Show card of the film

7

BLOOD, NOT TEARS!

A pall of gloom settled over the Chakravarty household, the moment Surendra was carried inside on a hospital stretcher. The childish prattle of Ajitha was heard no more. The girl, attending on her *dada*, looked older and more mature. The chubby, matronly mother, had aged overnight, and had developed white streaks in her hair. Even the cheerful expression of the deceased father in the photograph on the wall wore a somber look, which might possibly have been an effect of the layer of dust that had settled over the face. No one had time to dust the furniture and the pictures on the walls.

Surendra, lying on a low divan bed, looked wane and pale after what he had gone through in the lock-up. Added to the physical torture was a sense of guilt that he had failed his leader, betrayed his party and his comrades. He had broken down and blurted out the address of the party hideout and he could not excuse himself for this. He knew that others had been subjected to worse tortures but, still, they had not squealed, while he had told them everything. Yet it was not fear of death that had made him speak. He was not afraid of death. If he was hanged, or shot, he knew he would have cheerfully faced the prospect of death. But this was different. This was PAIN, excruciating, unbearable pain–the heel dug into his wound and not only pressed down but kept revolving, crushing his entrails and hurting the open, exposed nerves as if by a metallic meat-grinder. Why don't they shoot me?-The question had occurred to him in that agonised moment–but, at once, the answer came to him unasked. They were not killing him, for a dead man cannot talk, cannot betray their comrades. Torture was better because torture could get results. Torture was harder to bear than death which, in comparison and from the point of view of the victim, was infinitely preferable.

So they had tortured him, got what they wanted from him, and then sent him home to die–so they would not have his death on their hands. It wouldn't be "ANOTHER NAXALITE DIES IN LOCK-UP"!

But the family doctor who was called in to see him had declared that there was no chance for him to survive, it was just a matter of time, for the wound had become septic and the septicaemia had spread all over his body.

"Doctor Saheb, Doctor Saheb," Anand had asked him, running after him and talking to him in the outer verandah, "My friend will be all right, won't he?"

The doctor had just sadly shaken his head in the negative, patted Anand's shoulder gently and then slowly walked past him.

But when Anand went in, he had to lie to his friend and to his sister and his mother who sat by the side of her son, mute with grief and foreboding, "Don't speak, Surendra. The doctor has said that you will be all right soon, but that there should be no exertion on your part. The slightest strain will make your recovery difficult."

"No, Anand," Chakravarty spoke by the sheer exercise of his will power with difficulty, "I will not recover. I don't want to recover. Oh my God! I have told them everything. But I could not bear the torture any more, and could have betrayed my mother, my sister, my comrades, and betrayed them all...I deserve death–death–"

His voice, becoming weaker, trailed off into silence.

Anand could not bear it any longer, so he had to go and weep for the agony of his friend. He went out to the verandah.

Just then the inspector–the same man who had supervised the torture–entered through the *chik*, followed by a havildar.

"They must have another hideout. We must get this other address, too, out of him," the inspector was addressing his man, as he came in.

Anand looked up from the corner where he was sobbing. "I don't think he will be able to tell you anything–he is dying, as it is..."

The inspector was surprised to see the son of the deputy inspector general. "Must be college friends," he mused. But he made a note of it to inform Gangooly Saheb. Then he went in.

Anand also went in after him, if possible to save his friend further humiliation and agony.

After he was gone, two other young men–also from the Presidency College batch, entered the verandah. One of them had brought a long pistol wrapped in a newspaper.

They were Sinha, the Bihari, and Inder, the Bengali. Sinha was not sure they must kill their former comrade who had been their leader in college. But Inder was adamant, who answered "Those are the orders of the leader and the party. We have to carry them out! After all, he has betrayed us all–and the cause!"

Inside, the inspector was standing at the foot of Chkravarty's bed.

"You cheated us!" Anand heard him saying, "No one was there when we reached the address you gave us–you had somehow tipped them off. This is double-crossing, the punishment for which, you know, is death?" And he aimed his revolver at Chakravarty.

Chakravarty knew the inspector could not shoot him there and then. But he knew that, sooner or later, he would take him back to the police station and repeat the previous torture. But this time he was determined to deprive them of that *pleasure*. His hands were at last free. There was still some strength left in his long, bony fingers. He probed under the bandages, soon he found the wound-hole. He put his fingers in the wound and pressed them at the vital spot–till there was no strength left in them. He died of his own hand–without a bullet being fired by the inspector–or, outside, by the Naxalites who had come to shoot down a traitor who had betrayed their party!

The inspector put back his useless revolver in his holster and left casting a last glance at the DIG's son. What was he doing in the house of a Naxalite?

The Naxalites made their escape before the inspector walked out.

The mother, who had controlled herself before the police, now burst into a prolonged wailing and crying.

But the sister, Ajitha, who had taken her brother's dead, but bloodied, hand out of his wound, was grimly silent.

In that moment she raised her hand, covered with the blood of her brother, and silently looked long and hard at her blood-stained hand which was a symbol of her brother's sacrifice and called for some sort of revenge.

Anand, meanwhile, had sat down by his dead friend's side and surrendered himself to unabashed tears which were pouring from his eyes.

Ajitha saw him crying, ashamed of the weakness that he had demonstrated. She shook his shoulder to stop him, raised his chin to look into her eyes, then spoke with grim determination, "Look into my eyes, Anand. There are no tears–only blood!"

8

WHAT CAN YOU DO FOR REVOLUTION?

The face of Lenin, painted on a red poster, was serene and calm, while the face of Che Guevara was set in grim determination. "NAXALBARI-LAL SALAM" was emblazoned on the wall above these posters.

Both faces were on the walls of a room in North Calcutta, and Comrade Dada, who sat in front of Lenin's poster, was interrogating Ahitha, the sister of the dead Naxalite Surendra Chakravarty.

"Do you know what you will have to do for revolution?"

"I will have to live for revolution, I will have to die for revolution."

"If you are tortured, will you blurt out everything like your brother?"

"No, Comrade Dada. Whatever they do, I will not utter a single word."

"Do you know what they can do to a woman?"

"Yes, I know—but I will still not open my mouth."

"Who are our class enemies?" the question was abruptly put.

"Landlords, zamindars, money-lenders, forest contractors and big capitalists—these are our class enemies!"

"And who are our friends and comrades?"

"The socialists of the world are our friends and comrades–specially the peasants and workers of India!

"What can you sacrifice for the revolution?"

"My life–my honour!"

The rapid question-and-answer firing session ended with one last question, asked with slow deliberation.

"Is there a man whom you love?"

"No–if there was I would have no hesitation in sacrificing his love."

Anand who was standing in a corner, reacted to this question and answer.

But Comrade Dada was apparently satisfied with the answers given by Ajitha. Here was a girl with guts and spirits. He hoped she would prove stronger than her brother.

"*Achcha*!" he gave his verdict of approval, "We'll see. You live here for a couple of days–then we shall send you to do party work in some village!"

Ajitha went back to her place, gave a look of encouragement to Anand who was feeling nervous to face the cross-examination of Comrade Dada. It was his turn now. After exchanging silent glances with Ajitha, he went forward for the crucial confrontation with the old man.

"Who are you?" was the first question.

"Anand Kumar Gangooly."

"A name like some film star's. But we have no place for Kumars and Raj Kumars."

"Then you can call me just Anand."

"What does your father do?"

"*Ji?*" Anand knew the question would be asked–but betrayed his nervousness when answering it, "He–he–is a government officer."

"Tell us exactly what kind of officer is your father?"

"*Ji*—he is Deputy Inspector General—Reserve Police!"

The old man pondered the information before giving his verdict.

"Then I'm sorry—we cannot take you in the party! It can be dangerous!"

Pat came Anand's reply, "It can be dangerous—for your enemies!"

"You talk a lot—but how can we trust you?"

"If it is necessary for the cause of the revolution, I can even kill my father!" was his grim-faced reply.

"We don't want to encourage such murders," came Dada's reply, "What else can you do to prove your sincerity for the cause of revolution?"

"I can do this," and saying it, he took out a blade from his pocket and slashed his wrist with one stroke.

"These dramatics are unnecessary. But one test you will have to pass. Let's see whether you can do it or not?"

"I am prepared for any test, Comrade Dada. Tell me what I will have to do?"

"All right, we can admit you to our party if you can bring six bullets from the service revolver of your father this very night. This is the last time you have come in daylight! Henceforth you will only come during the night."

The service revolver was in the holster.

The holster was hanging from its belt over the uniform of the deputy inspector general.

The DIG was practicing his sitar, seated on the divan. He had reached an ecstatic moment of his *riyaaz*—so his eyes were closed as his fingers moved up and down on the strings.

Anand tip-toed into the room and, seeing his father's eyes closed as he practised his sitar, went straight to where the revolver was hanging on the clothes-rack, where he could see his father in the mirror.

To take out the revolver and to take the bullets out of the chamber was half a minute's work, but hardly had he put the bullets in his pocket than his father opened his eyes.

"Hello, Anand. I didn't know you were so interested in music. Sit down here," he indicated the divan and, after his son was seated, he went on, "It won't do you any harm–may even do some good!"

"Today you were absolutely wonderful, Baba. It appeared that you have captured the essence of music–the very soul of Gurudev," indicating the portrait of Tagore on the wall. "You should give a public concert one of these days."

Then he abruptly got up and walked out of the room, passing his mother on the way who was surprised to see her son emerging from his father's room.

"Sumitra," called out Gangooly, "did you hear that? Anand has begun to take interest in my music–was suggesting that I should give a public concert. That's a good sign, isn't it?"

The mother got a chance to defend her son. "You have always been prejudiced against our son! I told you he will come to the right path. Now, even you have to admit it. Come on, and have your dinner!" Then she suddenly remembered her son's habit of disappearing from the house, just as dinner was served on the table. She left her husband's room, calling "Anand, Anand!"

Anand was, indeed, on his way out when his mother's commanding voice caught up with him, and he was obliged to retrace his steps to the dining table.

The framed portrait of the DIG glared from the wall.

Under it, under his own shadow, as it were, sat Gangooly at his dinner table.

To his right sat his son, Anand, to his left sat his daughter, the teenaged Anamika, and right in front, facing him, sat his wife, Sumitra.

Everyone was silent but the teenaged daughter, a talkative schoolgirl, ventured to say something to her father. "Is it true that some students of Anand's college have been arrested?"

Gangooly was quick to answer, "Not *some* students. But *one* student"–emphasising that there was only one, "Surendra Chakravarty. Did you know him, Anand?"

"Yes, he was my friend!"

"Oh!" The DIG could not hide his surprise, "Then I am sorry to say that he is dead."

"I know," briefly put in Anand.

"How to you know?" It was not his father who was asking him a question but it was a police officer who was cross-examining him. "It's not yet in the papers!"

Now Anand had to blurt out the truth. "I was at his house when he died."

"Oh, I see!" There was sarcasm in Gangooly's voice.

Pushing away his plate, Anand got up, "Excuse me..."

"Sit down," his father ordered him, "and finish your dinner properly."

Anand spoke with bitterness in his emotion-charged voice. "I cannot eat anything when my friend has died a horribly painful death!" Then he added, making a direct reference to his father, "I cannot be like you!"

Gangooly sensed the implied attack on him. "What do you mean?" He did not ask, he shouted.

"That you can eat a six-course dinner, play Rabindra Sangeet on your sitar, while you know that your police officers are torturing brilliant young men in their torture cells–till they die!"

"Anand!" At last the mother intervened, "Is this the way to talk to your father?"

"I am going to my room," said Anand and he went inside, striding away from the dining room.

Both the mother and sister tried to stop Anand, but the father was quite calm. "Let him go! He is a little upset by his friend's death–a friend is a friend–even if he was a Naxalite!"

Mrs Gangooly, the mother of Anand and the wife of the deputy inspector general, was not able to sleep. While her husband peacefully slept–and snored–by her side.

She was still worrying about the conversation between the father and the son at the dining table, particularly about the violent altercation at the end. She had deep misgivings and forebodings about the future of her son.

It was past midnight when she heard a creak. From her sleeping position she tried to see in the dark whether it was a thief. But if it was a thief, it was an internal thief. For the door that had opened with the creak was the door of Anand's room. (His father, fearing the nocturnal propensities of a growing son had allotted him an inner room with the door opening into his own bedroom).

With horror Sumitra Gangooly saw her son entering on tip-toe. Where was he going at this hour? To a midnight rendezvous with a girl? She hoped it was so, for the other alternative was worse, and had in it the seeds of her son's destruction.

Anand tip-toed out of the parental bedroom, passing a few inches from his presumably sleeping mother. He could not see her expression in the faint moonlight that filled the room with deep shadows. But he could make out her sleeping form in the bed. He gently closed the outer door and was gone.

And his mother could not stop him or even question him about where he was going at that odd hour, for fear of awakening—and arousing the ire of—her husband. She merely worried—and wondered!

The little clock by the lampshade in Comrade Dada's room showed the time to be twenty minutes past midnight. He was still waiting for Anand to turn up with bullets from his father's revolver.

Of the two boys who were keeping the vigil with their leader, one spoke contemptuously, "He won't come, Dada! He is, after all, a coward—that son of the deputy inspector general!"

Just then, by one of those fateful synchronisations, there came a knock on the door.

"*Lal Salam*", came the code word. Dada recognised Anand's voice.

Dada smiled as he gestured to the boy to open the door.

Anand entered to be greeted by a less-than-cordial attitude.

"*We*," said Comrade Dada, indicating the young comrades, "thought you were not coming. Where are the bullets?"

"Here they are, Dada," replied Anand, producing from his pocket a handkerchief out of which he poured out six revolver bullets.

"Well done," said Dada, "I hope you had no difficulty in removing them."

"No, there was no difficulty in getting the bullets. Only some difficulty in getting out of the house."

"Then, tonight, you return home. But tomorrow bring a change of clothes when you come here after dark, for tomorrow night you sleep here and early next morning you leave for the villages—with the other comrades."

"I will do as you say—but not before I join the others in their 'postering'. Where can I find them?" He was excited about the experience of his first revolutionary assignment.

"They will be now in New Alipore," said Dada.

Across a wall in South Calcutta—a big white lettering appeared: VICTORY TO THE NAXALITE PATH, painted by Anand. Near him was Ajitha with a pail of white paint.

Anand was busy putting the finishing touches to the big lettering when a boy, told to watch out for the police shouted, "Police! Police!!"

All the four Naxalite boys putting up Naxalite posters and slogans in the vicinity ran post-haste but by the time Anand had finished his lettering, and Ajitha had hidden her pail of paint in a nearby gutter, they almost ran into a pot-bellied havildar in white uniform.

Anand had no time to think but, on the spur of the moment, he decided to pretend to be a drunk propositioning a girl—presumably a street-walker.

"Come on, my dear!" He put conviction into his theatrical words as he pulled Ajitha to his side, "I tell you I love you very, very much. I tell you I love you more than my life."

The havildar was soon questioning him, "Eh, Sir, have you seen some Naxalites putting up posters?"

His reply, for a moment, almost stunned Ajitha, for he said, "Yeah—yeah—I have seen them. They are here," indicating the pocket of his kurta, "but they are also there!" pointing to the posters on the wall. Then he spoke directly to the policeman.

"Come here, havildar!" adding a confidential tone to his whispered words.

The havildar came forward hopefully, expecting to get vital information.

But he said to him, "Tell this girl to come with me. She thinks that I am drunk and I won't pay her anything. So she won't come with me. Tell her I will give her a hundred *rupeesh*...even a thousand *rupeesh*—just for one night."

The havildar agreed to be the go-between between the ardent lover and the reluctant girl. "Eh, girl, why don't you go with this Saheb? He has a big heart and will give you much money."

"Ah, money? That reminds me. You deserve this for your efforts on behalf of Love, Havildar Saheb." And he pressed a ten-rupee note into the not-unwilling hand of the police head constable.

"Thank you, Sir. Thank you very much. But, you better go home. Beware of the Naxalites. They put up these subversive posters and throw bombs on peace-loving people including policemen."

Then, with a respectful salute to the "Saheb", the policeman walked away, looking for Naxalites.

Arm in arm with the *girl*, Anand walked in another direction. But, after some yards, he let go of her hand.

"I am sorry," he said, suddenly self-conscious and apologetic for his play-acting, "That's the only thing I could think of."

"That was all make-believe, was it not?" There was a merest note of regret in her answer, "All that you were saying before the policeman came."

"I must apologise for the way I said it, but it was all true."

"But, Anand, in our party we have no love-life. We are all married..."

He interjected before she could finish the sentence.

"Married? Married to whom?"

"Married to Death!" She completed the sentence.

It was a warning–and a premonition!

The atmosphere at the Gangoolys' breakfast table was as tense as the expression on Gangooly's face in the portrait was grim.

The DIG was reading one of the banned papers of the Naxalites.

Anand was silently playing with his pen, while his sister had her eyes on it. The mother was watching them all in silence.

At last the teenaged sister broke the silence.

"Dada," she said addressing her elder brother, "If you are tired of this old pen, please give it to me."

Her brother threw the pen across the breakfast table. "Take it. I know it is useless thing, anyway. One needs something else in one's hands."

The sister didn't understand it, but the mother reacted with a sudden change of expression. What on earth was her son talking about?

But Anamika went on chattering in her schoolgirl manner. "Oh, thank you Dada. When I show it off in school, all the girls will be so jealous!"

"Anamika!" Her mother admonished her. "Don't you see your father is reading the newspaper, and doesn't want to be disturbed?"

Mr Gangooly abruptly crumpled the newspaper in his hand in a violent gesture.

Anamika wanted an immediate explanation, "Is there some bad news in the paper, Baba?"

"It's all bad news. What else do you expect in a Naxalite newspaper? These bastards have become a chronic nuisance!"

The table spoon fell from Anand's hand onto the plate, with a clatter, as he got up abruptly from his chair.

"What's it?" Mr Gangooly asked him, "Have you suddenly developed some sympathy with these hooligans?"

"If they are bastards, then I want to tell you that there is a bastard in your own family too."

Without raising his voice Mr Gangooly asked, "Who is he?"

"*I* am that bastard!" replied Anand in a tone of finality.

"Anand!" His mother was shocked. "Have you gone mad? Do you know what you are saying–you are abusing *yourself*–your father–your mother!"

Anand went on, "I only know that I am what they are! Their way is my way, their ideals–and their ideology–are mine also. What they do, I do. So I am going–to them!"

He had started to go when his mother's words forced him to turn back. "How can you go, Anand? We have made all arrangements for your marriage with a very beautiful girl."

But that was a bait that he would not even look at. "Ma! You keep your *beautiful girl* with you. I am already married!"

"Without our permission?" She shouted. "How can that be?"

And his father asked, "To whom?"

Anand gave a two-word reply, "To Death!"

And his receding footsteps had an ominous, foreboding echo of finality.

The mother was now crying helplessly and piteously.

"Enough of it, Sumitra. Your son isn't dead yet!" Then he shouted a command.

"Sher Singh!"

A burly squat man, with a cap on his shaven head, stood and saluted him at the door, "Yes, Sir."

"Follow him!" He indicated the way his son had gone out, and the plain-clothes policeman saluted again and was gone.

"This time I have made fool-proof arrangement to bring back your errant son. One sub-inspector and two havildars in a jeep will follow wherever Anand goes–so by the evening, we will raid the hide out of the Naxalites and bring back your son."

The mother tried to smile between her tears. "True?" she asked, hoping and believing!

Anand walked aimlessly–trying to kill time before nightfall, when, only, he was supposed to go to the secret house in North Calcutta where Dada would meet him and give him instructions about carrying the message of revolution to the villages.

Since he had left home abruptly, without a warning, he did not know that a jeep was following him at a discreet distance.

He went into the New Alipore Park to spend a few hours, reading a revolutionary pamphlet that Ajitha had given him. He found a convenient spot, an empty bench under a shady tree. There he lay down and started reading the pamphlet from page one. The title of the pamphlet was: "Fathers and Sons".

The jeep had followed him to the park gate, and was waiting.

The sun was setting over Calcutta when he finished reading the pamphlet. It was an exhortation to sons and fathers alike. Anand wished that he could make his father go through it, though he knew him too well to expect anything to come out of it!

He got up from the park bench, yawned to shake off the stiffness of his body, then he carefully folded the pamphlet—which was Ajitha's first gift to him—and put it back in his pocket. Then he started walking out through a side gate.

It was then that he saw Ramona coming in. She was a class fellow of his, a girl from a rich business family who had long cast her eyes on Anand and taken every opportunity to win over the DIG's son who (her status-conscious mother had told her) would be a good *catch*.

She was entering through the iron grills of the side gate. The moment she saw him, she lovingly "helloed" him. Anand always thought her a bore and a pest, but since she was coming in through the gate, there was no way to escape her.

"Hello, Anand," she said, flashing her smile.

"Hello, Ramona." It was clear that he was less than enthusiastic about meeting her. But she was not to be discouraged.

"Have been missing you at college these days. Professor Verma was asking about you. Hope you have been well."

"I am quile well," Anand brusquely replied, "Just don't feel like coming to college these days!"

"I hope you haven't joined the Naxalite gang?" She asked, making it quite clear that she did not like them.

"Who? Me a Naxalite! I am not worthy of being a Naxalite!" That way he was not talking a lie, while also not revealing his membership of the party.

He made a move to go but Ramona thrust out her manicured hand to catch the bars of the gate to make his sudden exit impossible.

"It's so difficult to find you," she was saying, "Now that I have found you, I was hoping you would take me to a restaurant for a cup of tea. Then we can go to a 6:30 pm show. I have two tickets."

"No, no, I have an important appointment somewhere at that time. Some other day we will go to the pictures."

Ramona was a leech and she was difficult to get rid of! "I can give you another chance. It's a very good picture–full of emotion and suspense."

Anand had to ask, "What is the name of the picture?"

She replied, "*Tomorrow Never Comes*".

Anand had to walk nearly two miles through the dense returning-from-office traffic. He knew that once again he would be late and hoped he would not be reprimanded. He also hoped he would have a chance of seeing Ajitha before he left on his rural assignment. It would be too much of a good thing if she was also accompanying them to the villages–but, in the corner of his heart, there was that hope.

He was so full of thoughts of Ajitha that he did not notice the jeep that was still following him.

Ajitha and her comrades of yesterday were being interrogated by Comrade Dada.

"You are sure you were not followed by the police yesterday? I have told you so many times that even if you have the slightest suspicion you are to avoid coming here!"

"Comrade Dada, we made absolutely sure we were not followed by any one. But we can't say about Anand, for he stayed on at the place. From a distance we saw him talking to a havildar. He was certainly not arrested."

Ajitha intervened to come to his defence. "He was almost arrested. But he pretended to be a drunkard trying to proposition me. That's how I was also saved."

A hard note crept into Dada's voice, "That puts the suspicion on you, too, Ajitha."

Ajitha faced the leader with resolute equanimity. "I'll do anything to remove the suspicion."

"Will you?" Dada asked a simple and short question—but Ajitha knew it was the voice of doom.

"Yes, I will," she replied.

Dada turned to Shankar, perhaps the youngest of his boys.

"Shankar, you go out and hide in the bushes at the entrance of the lane. Keep a watch. If Anand comes here, followed by a party of plain-clothes policemen—you recognise the type -then blow a sharp whistle to warn us—you know it, of course."

The young boy said, "Of course, Dada," and blew a whistle to satisfy his leader.

"Then we will immediately go off by the back door—meet us at the other place. You all get out now. We can't take the risk of being arrested together."

The three Naxalites left and Ajitha got up to go with them.

"You sit down here," ordered Dada, and Ajitha sat down, resigned to her fate.

By the time Anand got to the lane leading to Dada's secret headquarters, he was really tired. It had been a long and dusty tramping through thick traffic, dodging cars and buses. He had money to take a taxi to cut short the walk, but that was not allowed in the party. Moreover, it was the tainted money which his father had given him—and he knew it came from the government for doing his duty—which included catching and torturing and killing Naxalites!

Slowly he walked down the lane—but to Shankar, ordered to keep a watch on him, it looked as if he was walking furtively.

Before he took the last turning, he looked back to make sure he was not followed. That is what he had been taught. But tonight it acquired another meaning when, after Anand had gone in, a jeep silently pulled up at the end of the lane, stopped there, its lights switched off, and three men got down from it, and started to follow stealthily.

Shankar blew the sharp warning whistle.

The whistle was heard in the room like the bugle of doom.

Dada's once-handsome features were contorted with tension, for he had to take a grim decision.

He turned to Ajitha. "You will be able to do it?"

"Yes, Dada," she said briefly, grimly.

"Then, take this–" he said, offering her his own pistol.

He had already instructed her what she had to do–in case the warning whistle sounded.

She had to open the door with her left hand, holding the pistol at her eye level. The moment Anand was to enter, she had to press the trigger. That's all! As simple as that. After that she had to run for the back exit and join the other Naxalites.

She opened the door, saw a look of puzzled bewilderment on Anand's handsome face.

Tears were brimming over in her eyes. But she pulled the trigger hard. There was a flash and an explosion both within and without her.

The pistol, its—and her—duty done, fell uselessly at her feet—floating down in slow motion. In slow motion, too, she saw Anand—*her* Anand, the Anand whom it was a pleasure to feed *luchi-tarkari*, for whom she would hum lines from Tagore—that same Anand fall down, at her feet—his face a crimson pulp of flesh and blood.

She had done her duty as a Naxalite.

Now she was a young woman in love—though she had killed her lover with her own hands.

She sat down and took Anand's head into her lap.

He cast a wistful last glance at her, out of his bloody, pulpy, fleshy mouth came a whispered question: "*Kyon*, Ajitha, *kyon* (Why, Ajitha, why)?" Then he died in her lap.

But the question that he had asked would echo in Ajitha's ears till her own dying day—it would assume loud and urgent proportions which would make it audible above the crash of bullets and bombs, and the fatal creaking of the gallows as the plank would be mechanically moved away beneath her feet:

Why?

Why?

WHY?

WHY?

9

BLOOD-BROTHERS!

The wheel of the cycle-rickshaw went round and round—like the eternal cycle of life.

Raghoo, a tall but frail young man, was pedaling the cycle-rickshaw, dragging a fat man with his luggage, from the station to his home.

He went along the main roads.

He went along the side roads.

He went through traffic.

He went through the maze of lanes and by-lanes, till he came to his destination.

The fat man insisted on Raghoo lifting his heavy trunk and carrying it to his second-floor flat.

Raghoo agreed to it, hoping to get an extra tip. He struggled, he heaved and panted, till he carried the trunk to the second floor.

Then he extended his palm to receive—a 50-paise coin, That was the fare as well as the tip. With that coin in his hand, he went to look for a cup of tea.

At a restaurant...

Raghoo was stopped at the entrance. He was an untouchable, a pariah, he could not enter the place.

He only wanted tea.

So he was given a metal glass tied to a chair that was lying outside.

Into that, a glass of tea was poured in a very conspicuously insulting manner. The money was accepted very patronisingly, but carefully, so that his palm should not touch the hand of the manager.

Again the cycle of life went round and round.

Now Raghoo was slow, because he was tired. He coughed and he spat out–*blood*!

But he went on pulling the rickshaw.

Now he was going along the *bund*–a wide, smooth road–and a fashionable husband and wife were seated in his pedi-cab.

A swarm of cycles–college boys and girls were pedalling, on their way to a picnic.

They taunted the rickshaw puller.

The man and woman urged him to hurry up to catch up with them. Some of the cycling fraternity were known to them. They didn't want to be left behind.

Raghoo went faster and faster–

Till he was abreast with the freewheeling cycles.

On the other side came an aristocrat's phaeton.

Now Raghoo was not only racing against the cycles–but also against the sturdy horses of the phaeton.

Sometimes he was seen through the wheels of the freewheeling cycles.

Sometimes the phaeton and the horses were seen through his rickshaw wheels–

The horse's hoofs.

The painful pedalling of Raghoo.

The lusty, joyous freewheeling cycles.

It became a triangle of movement and rhythm.

The circles of cycle wheels.

The hoofs of the horses.

The pedalling legs of Raghoo.

Till at last Raghoo could not keep it up.

Everything went hazy–

Everything went crazily topsy-turvy.

Everything collapsed.

But actually only Raghoo's cycle-rickshaw had collapsed.

He was lying on the road–in a pool of blood–his own blood. Blood that he had vomited.

Raghoo was brought in on a stretcher to the emergency ward.

Doctor Rao looked at the X-ray of Raghoo's lungs and a frown appeared on his face.

"Great loss of blood," was his verdict, "He has TB too, though it is still the first stage."

"It is the old, old story of rickshaw-pullers–probably the seventeenth that I have witnessed during my six months here."

He said it to Ashraf Ali, a young man who was his junior doctor; he was a fresh medical graduate.

"What is to be done, Doctor?"

"Blood transfusion!" The doctor declared, "But the supply of free plasma is finished–no new stocks expected for a month–who would give his blood for this poor wretch?"

"I will, Doctor."

"Your blood group must match!"

"It matches already. His group, we have found is RI—the same as mine."

"Then we must hurry up. It will have to be a direct transfusion! There is no time to lose."

The unconscious Raghoo felt new strength pouring into his body.

He opened his eyes. And he saw a rubber tube joining him to a young man of his own age lying on another bed close by.

Ashraf Ali smiled at the sight of Raghoo opening his eyes.

Raghoo smiled back at him, forgetting for the moment the difference in their status.

A calendar sheet is torn off to indicate the passage of days.

Raghoo was now sufficiently recovered to be let out of the hospital.

Doctor Ashraf Ali gave him instructions to take milk every day, and wholesome food, and he gave him the medicines to take with him.

"Come to me if there is any trouble. Come on, I will see you off," said Ashraf.

The doctor accompanied Raghoo to the compound of the hospital where his broken cycle-rickshaw was standing.

Raghoo happily sat on the saddle and pedalled away, after saying goodbye to Dr Ashraf Ali.

Prafulla Reddy was the owner of Raghoo's cycle-rickshaw. He was also the owner of several dozen other cycle-rickshaws. He also owned the men like Raghoo who plied these rickshaws for him.

He looked like a cinema villain–with sword-cut moustaches. He also behaved in the same callous manner.

"Eh, you bastard, where have you been all these days?" he used this vulgar language while talking to these men.

"Saheb, I was in a hospital. See this is the *satificate* that the Doctor Saheb has given me."

He handed the letter to Reddy.

Reddy read it, then contemptuously said to his henchmen and other rickshaw-pullers, "Look what this *Musallah* doctor says: Certified that Raghoo son of Ramoo of village Jagirpur, has been under treatment at this hospital for the last eight days. He is being discharged now, but he should be given light work and wholesome diet including two glasses of milk and one egg every day." Then he tore and threw the letter aside. "So I am to give this *haramkhore* two glasses of milk, chicken curry and what not? Also give him light work. But who will compensate me for one week's rent of my cycle-rickshaw?" To Raghoo he said, "You, bastard? Or your *Musallah* doctor? Speak up, you swine! And who will pay for the repairs of this cycle-rickshaw that you have broken in some drunken brawl?"

After a while he said, "Come on, sign this here."

"What is it?" Raghoo asked, with new audacity in him.

"So you dare to ask me, your employer, what is to be signed? All right, I'll tell you–it is eight days rent plus the cost of repairs. You sign this document so that till you pay it off, you will have to work here for free."

Raghoo looked around and found impassive faces of the other rickshaw-pullers.

He signed it.

At night in the barrack-like room, where Raghoo occupied a corner along with other rickshaw-pullers, he lay awake.

"Say, brother, were you treated by a *Musallah* doctor, as the Contractor Saheb said?"

"Yes, the doctor was a Muslim. Do you know he saved my life by giving his own blood. So I have Muslim blood in my veins now. I saw that it was also red—just like my blood."

"Why did you sign that paper?" One of his companions asked. "Now, you will never escape his clutches!"

"Is that so?"

"Yes—he made us all sign such papers and now we are all his slaves."

"Run away," one advised, in a whisper.

"Run away," hissed another.

"Run away," said a third.

In the dark night Raghoo ran away.

He went straight to the hospital. In the morning, Ashraf Ali, when he came on duty, found him sleeping on the bench outside.

"Eh, Raghoo, what are you doing here?" asked Ashraf.

Raghoo got up and explained. "The Contractor Saheb made me sign a paper. And then all said, 'Run away, Run away!', so I ran away."

"It's the old, old story. Have you eaten anything?"

"No, Doctor Saheb, I had only a handful of rice last night."

"All right." And he rang the bell. A peon entered. "Bring two plates of *idli* and two cups of coffee for us. Quick."

Then he attended to some of his work. Meanwhile, the peon brought the cups of coffee and the *idlis*.

"Come on, Raghoo, eat."

Ranghoo hesitated, then said, "Doctor Saheb, I am an untouchable."

"So what? Being your blood-brother, then I must be also an untouchable. Come on, eat–who told you are an untouchable?"

"I always knew I was an untouchable. But then a tea-shop owner reminded me that I was an untouchable..."

In the evening, Ashraf Ali took Raghoo to his house.

On the way they passed the restaurant where Raghoo was insulted.

The place was in shambles. The furniture and the crockery had been broken down and the broken pieces were lying on the road.

"What happened, Seth?" Ashraf Ali asked, apparently solicitously.

"The Naxalites had been here. It is all their handiwork. How was I to know that that untouchable was a Naxalite?"

He went and complained to his party and look what they have done to my place!"

Raghoo smiled at this.

But he asked Ashraf Ali later, "Brother, tell me who are the Naxalites?"

"They are people who don't take injustice and cruelty lying down, they hit back at all reactionaries and tyrants."

"Then I would like to meet them," said Raghoo, "I would like to be one of them."

"You will, tonight."

Ashraf Ali's wife, a pretty young woman, was offering *namaz* when they entered the place.

Ashraf Ali's house was full of books–not only medical books but books on politics and revolution.

There were also posters on the wall—Mao Tse-tung, Che Guevara, Charu Mazumdar, etc.

Then he met Mrs Ashraf Ali, she was a pious young woman, but with fire in her eyes.

"Meet my comrade and brother Raghoo," Ashraf introduced his companion.

He folded his hands.

She *salamed* him, gave him a clean towel to wash his hands and face.

Then she spread the *dastarkhwan* and Ashraf forced Raghoo to eat with him.

"But you are a Mussalman, aren't you?"

"Yes, what does it mean?"

"I thought Mussalmans never eat with untouchables!"

In his eyes there was a remembrance of what happened many years ago...

The cycle of life revolved...

But it was not the wheel of a cycle, or a cycle-rickshaw.

But the wheel of a buggy in which the Jagirdar Rahat Jung, was inspecting his estates. All his peasants were standing on both sides of the village road in Telangana.

One such peasant was holding his son on his shoulder, the son was Raghoo. So was the recollection of his father.

Because he was using his right hand to hold his son on his shoulder, the father was unable to lift both his hands to namaskar the jagirdar.

The jagirdar noticed this lapse on the part of one of his peasants, and stopped the buggy-driver.

"*Thairo*," he shouted, his big moustaches quivering with anger.

The buggy stopped near Raghoo and his father.

The child, unconcerned, felt happy and even smiled. He clapped his hands.

The jagirdar ordered the coachman who came down from the buggy.

"Haven't you got hands to salute?" he asked.

"*Huzoor*, I was holding up my son with one hand."

"Your son means more to you than Jagirdar Saheb?" the coachman shouted at him and then began whipping him with the coachman's leather whip.

Raghoo's father put down the son on the ground, but meanwhile he had already received a few lashes along with the father.

The taste of those lashes and the agony of his father as he lay on the ground, receiving lashes after lashes was still fresh in the memory of Raghoo.

Ashraf Ali asked Raghoo, "Then what happened to your father?"

Raghoo proudly told him, "When the Telangana movement started he joined the guerillas and was hanged six months later, after a battle with the police, but while dying he left his gun to be given to my mother. She has kept it hidden in her room to be used by me, his son, when the time comes."

Raghoo and his mother stood outside the jail wall while the father was being hanged. "The time will come," his mother grimly remarked as the time of hanging arrived.

"The time has come now," said Ashraf Ali.

Just then there was a knock on the door and when he opened it, three men entered and, looking about, closed the door.

"This is Comrade Reddy," said Ashraf Ali.

"This is Comrade Babu," he said pointing to the next newcomer.

"This is Comrade Anwarul Haq. He is from Calcutta," he said pointing to the third man with a small beard.

"Reddy is the new landlord of our village," said Raghoo.

"There is nothing in a name–your first landlord was Rahat Jung, you now have a Reddy–they are both the same. One Babu may be a rogue, another Babu might be a comrade. Anwarul Haq may be a zamindar's henchman–or he might be the liquidator of landlords and their henchmen," pointing to the third one.

"They are the ones who wrecked that restaurant whose manager had insulted you–and other untouchables."

"Thank you, sirs–comrades. Why did you take the trouble?"

"It was no trouble. It was a pleasure," said Anwarul Haq. "We had to do something to prove our bonafides to you."

"What does it mean?"

Dr Ashraf replied, "That you are now one of us–and you are going to your village to get back our gun. But I won't be going with you. I am to remain here. You four will go."

"When?"

"Now," said Reddy.

A road transport bus, raising clouds of dust, came to a stop somewhere in the countryside of Telangana.

Four of them came out–Raghoo, accompanied by Reddy, Anwarul Haq and Babu.

Now they walked, after the bus was gone.

By the time they reached the village it was dark.

Raghoo found his door, knocked on it.

His mother opened the door, saw her son, was happy, embraced him, but was puzzled by the three strangers with him. She even thought they were the police or the CID men. When he asked for his father's gun, she asked, "Who are they?"

"They are my comrades, Mother. So, first give us something to eat."

The mother looked at them once more. Then she smiled, and enquired in a whisper, "Naxalites?"

Raghoo silently nodded.

She put something to eat before them.

Then she went into her room and from a box took out a double-barrel gun.

She brought it out, took it before an altar where the gods and goddesses were placed beside a flickering *chiragh*, she placed *kumkum* on the gun. Then she handed it to her son who placed it on his head.

"Comrades," he said, "now I am one of you–a Naxalite!"

"But your *nishana* must be correct," said one of the comrades.

"First I must return to Hyderabad. I have a debt to pay there."

The contractor was sipping country liquor from a glass alone in his room.

Suddenly the door was flung open. Entered Raghoo, now looking like a "black devil of vengeance".

"So it's you! What do you want?"

"Nothing, Contractor Saheb. I am going on a war. And one can't go on a holy war without paying one's debts. I have come to pay my debts."

"To whom?" The contractor asked, puzzled as well as worried.

"To you"–and, from behind him, he withdrew his double-barrel gun.

He took careful aim.

The contractor, a coward, cringed before Raghoo.

"Anything that you want?"

"Then give me that paper that you got signed by me."

The contractor rummaged in his desk and brought out the paper. He handed it to Raghoo.

Raghoo showed it to Reddy. "Comrade, see that it is the correct one."

Reddy looked at the paper and nodded, "Yes, it is correct."

"Give me all such papers."

The contractor gave him the papers.

Raghoo lit them with a little flame of the matchstick which became a big flame.

10

THE HONOUR OF A SANTHAL

An apple was put on the head of Thekedar Ghanshyam Singh, with his arrogant moustaches.

Kanu, a young Santhal, split the apple with one arrow.

Kanu Santhal was dancing happily. Because he had won the contest and found the girl after his heart.

She was Rambha! A seventeen-year-old girl, new to their village.

But two other eyes were focused on the youthful body of Rambha. They were the eyes of Ghanshyam, the new forest contractor who was sitting on a chair, watching the welcome dance that had been arranged in his honour.

As the rhythm of the dance slackened, the thekedar asked one of his henchmen, pointing to Rambha, "Who is that girl?"

"She is Rambha, daughter of Sankara, a tribal, landless peasant. He is famous for his drinking!"

"Then call him to my bungalow—we will give him a bottle of drink."

The woodcutting in the forest was going on. The sturdy—and *black*—Kanu was wielding his powerful axe on a gash in the tree.

One more strike and the tree was ready to fall.

It was falling–falling–right on top of Rambha who was sitting down in the shade on a stump of a tree, playing with *mahua* flowers.

The tree would have fallen on her but for the timely intervention of Kanu, who ran to her, clutched her hand and dragged her out of harm's way.

Behind her, the heavy tree fell with an alarming thud.

But she was unafraid–not in a panic at all. She had something else on her mind.

"Do you know what it means to catch a girl by the hand?" she asked Kanu.

Kanu smiled and his teeth flashed in the sunlight. "Yes, I know–it means that he is going to be her man!"

Now, she too smiled. "I thought you were only trying to save me from the falling!" she pouted.

"That also!" answered Kanu. "It would have been disastrous if the tree had fallen on you–"

"Not so bad–if we had been together."

"Is that so?"

"Yes," she said and ran away. "I wouldn't mind dying with you. Then, I would know that in the next birth, too, you would be my man."

"*Aray*, first talk of this life! Then we will worry about the next."

"Have you thought of this life?" And Kanu laughed happily while Rambha started plucking the branches of the tree.

"Hey!" came the voice of the thekedar's henchman, "What are you doing?"

"I am chopping the branches of the tree, and that's my man who has chopped it down with his axe. It is my right."

"Is he your man?" asked the thekedar's henchman.

"Is she your woman?" The henchman asked of Kanu.

"Yes, she is."

"Strange," commented the henchman, "Your father says you are still a virgin."

"I won't be a virgin tonight. We are going to the *gotul* tonight, aren't we Kanu?"

"Yes, we are," he replied, defiantly contemptuous of this burly body whom the thekedar had sent.

The father was sitting outside his hut, already half-drunk when the henchman came to see him.

"Come on, the Thekedar Saheb is waiting for you with the bottle!"

The old man was ready to go immediately.

"But," the henchman asked him, "How will you come back? It will be night-time and you may stumble in the forest. Better take someone to be with you. Take your son, maybe." He said in wily and oily tones.

"I have no son," Rambha's father said innocently. "I have only a daughter."

"Rambha!" The father called.

Inside, Rambha was doing her *sringar* to go to the *gotul* with Kanu.

"Yes, father."

"Come with me to the Thekedar Saheb's bungalow," he commanded her, "You will have to bring me back through the forest."

"But, father," she feebly protested, "I have to go to the *gotul* with Kanu."

"You did not tell me," the father said feebly, "How am I to know that you have started going to the *gotul* with a young man?"

"I haven't started going!" Rambha corrected him, "I am going for the first time tonight."

"*Aray*, come out—first comes the duty to your father, then you can go anywhere with anyone of your choice—if you still want to go with a good-for-nothing fellow like Kanu—after meeting the Thekedar Ghanshyam Singh!"

"I don't care for your Thekedar," said Rambha, "But I will come for my father's sake."

As she accompanied her father, she called out to her neighbor, "*Aray*, Kallo, listen! If Kanu comes to take me to the *gotul*, then tell him I am going with my father to the Thekedar's place. I will be back in one hour. Let him wait here for me!"

A friend of Kanu, hearing splashing inside, called out, "*Aray*, Kanu, what are you doing?"

"I am washing my whole body."

"The whole body? What, what's the matter?" The friend asked in surprise.

"I am going to the *gotul* with Rambha tonight," replied Kanu.

Then he came out, all dressed up for the occasion to bring his bride to the *gotul*.

On the way to Rambha's hut, passing the *gotul* he told the giggling girls and the laughing boys that he would soon be back with his Rambha.

When Kanu reached Rambha's house, he called for her, she was not there.

Her neighbor, also a saucy young woman named Shanti tried to entice him. "Your Rambha has gone with her father to the Thekedar's place, she will not be a virgin when she comes back. But I am also a virgin, why not take me to the *gotul*?"

Kanu, hearing of the lecherous thekedar, was already striding alone through the forest, carrying his staff with him.

On the way he encountered a furious hyena and killed it with his staff which had a metalled end.

The hyena's blood was on the edge of his staff as he reached the thekedar's house.

Rambha's father was lying dead-drunk in a corner, while the thekedar was trying, first, to entice Rambha, then to drag her and coerce her, but she would not yield. "My virginity is the *amanat* of Kanu. It is not for sale," she said.

Kanu, the Santhal, challenged the thekedar.

The thekedar took out a revolver and shot at Kanu.

The bullet grazed Kanu's arm but he had already hit Ghanshyam Singh with his staff and felled him.

Taking Rambha by the arm, he fled from there.

In the *gotul*, a corner was allowed to Kanu and Rambha.

It was here that Rambha bandaged Kanu's arm, applying the medicinal paste of some herbs ground down on a stone.

After that, they made love.

Then they slept–like two innocent children clasped together.

In the morning when they got up, the police was already

there in a jeep to arrest Kanu on the charge of assaulting the thekedar.

In vain did Rambha protest, she told the story of how the whole thing came about–how the thekedar was bent on dishonouring her–how he shot at Kanu when he tried to save her–but the police wouldn't listen to her. They had a complaint, and they had to make an arrest.

Rambha tried to run after the jeep in which her Kanu sat, but was left standing in the forest as the jeep sped away, enveloped by the cloud of dust that the jeep raised.

At the police station, Kanu was told that if he happened to kill the man who was in the same lock-up he would be released, and then he could go back to his Rambha. Otherwise that man would kill Kanu.

Then Kanu was pushed into the lock-up, where one other man was already lying down wounded (he had been tortured).

There was suspense as the sturdy tribal stood menacingly over the frail and tortured political prisoner.

He got up when Kanu entered, ready to fight back, for ruffians were introduced into his cell to make mince-meat of him.

Kanu did not understand why the other man was hostile to him.

"Why?" he simply asked him in his tribal dialect.

"Aren't you sent to beat me?"

"No. Why should I beat you?"

"Because I am supposed to be a Naxalite."

"What is a Naxalite?" The tribal, who was illiterate, did not understand political jargon, so he asked.

The man understood his ignorance. He did not explain that the communist party had three main divisions and his Marxist-Leninist party was the latest and the most dynamic.

He only said, "Because I am a friend of the poor–because I don't believe in the poor taking their sufferings at the hands of exploiters like zamindars, capitalists and the forest thekedars lying down."

Kanu understood one name–thekedars.

"I know one Thekedar Ghanshyam Singh. He tried to spoil my wife. I hit out at him. He shot me in the arm," and indicated the wound on his arm. "Still the police arrested me–not him."

"I will tell you why?"

The Naxalite said, "Come, and sit down. So we can talk comfortably."

The police officers shouted why the Naxalite was not being beaten.

Kanu pretended to hit the Naxalite and the policemen were smiling in their office.

The Naxalite and the tribal talked till dawn.

The Naxalite said, "So you see there is nothing to be afraid of. At most they can kill you. But people like us are always ready to die. You must remember one thing. The strength of the poor people–the landless labourers, the tribals, the workers–is in their unity. If all of your people had stood up, no one could have dared to arrest you!"

That Kanu understood.

He nodded his head.

The Naxalite who was already half-dead, died after talking.

One Naxalite was dead and another was born.

Then the cell door opened and the policeman came in and saw the dead Naxalite. "Come on, Kanu son of Ramaya. You have to appear in court."

Before leaving, Kanu touched the feet of the dead Naxalite. The policeman said, "*Shabash*, you have done well to kill him."

In court they asked him if it was true that, armed with a lethal weapon, he entered the thekedar's house with intent to rob him.

"No."

"Then, what were you doing there?"

"He was trying to molest my wife, so I went to protect her."

The lawyer said, "Rambha is not your wife."

"Before the gods, and according to the laws of our tribe, and by her free consent, she *is* my wife!"

"Here is the statement of Sankara, the father of Rambha. He says he never married his daughter to you!"

"*Huzoor*," said the tribal youth, "I married his daughter, not the old man Sankara. Why don't you ask her?"

At that there was laughter in court.

The magistrate said, "Order! Order!"

Then the magistrate said to the accused, "You are a tribal. But you speak like a Naxalite."

"I *am* a Naxalite!"

"Two year's rigorous imprisonment," declared the magistrate.

When Kanu was in the prison cell he heard a big noise and many slogans. He climbed on to something to reach the window. He saw through the bar window a big crowd standing and shouting that they would burn the police station if the body of Sambha Naxalite was not handed over to them.

Meanwhile, a warder happened to come and Kanu asked him what the noise was about.

The warder told him that it was about the Naxalite troublemaker who had died last night at the hands of Kanu, and now peasants were demanding his body to take out a procession.

The warder told him that he was a leader of the landless peasants and was harassing the landlords and threatening them. "He was really a dacoit just like you."

The warder left and Kanu muttered "Just like *me*—just like *me*!"

From outside came the voices of the crowd, *"Sambha Zindabad!" "Ssambha Amar Rahey"*.

Again he climbed to the barred window and saw through the bars the procession of the peasants going away with the dead body of Sambha.

There was a bright new expression on the face of Kanu. He knew now what he would do in the future.

11

RAINBOW OF HAPPINESS

At last his two years of imprisonment was over. He came out of jail—a little thinner but with more marks of intelligence on his face.

First he went through the fields to the village of Sambha and enquired about Sambha's *samadhi*. The villagers pointed out to a grave around which a fencing of bamboo was put on. Kanu went there and offered his homage.

He was told that, often, the police came and broke down the bamboo fencing and the *samadhi* of Sambha, again, it was restored by the villagers. For the real *samadhi* was in their hearts and that the police could not touch or even reach.

Then Kanu went to his own village, straight to the house of Rambha. Her father was drinking, as usual.

"Where is my wife?" He asked.

"Died of drowning!"

"You are lying—you sold her to the Thekedar, for a few bottles of liquor?"

"No, I didn't. Believe me, son."

He spoke with a new softness and compassion in his voice, yet he was drunk. "Now this bottle is my only companion."

So Kanu turned to Rambha's neighbor, Kallo.

She started crying in reply.

Then she spoke, "After some months of your imprisonment, the Thekedar waylaid her in the forest one day. He raped her and the next day she committed suicide by drowning in a well."

There was a grim expression on the face of Kanu.

"But there is a souvenir she has left for you!"

She went inside and brought out a year-old child, black like his father, but with the chiseled features of his mother.

"This is your son–your son and her son!"

He declined to take him. "Keep him for a while," he implored her, "I have a debt to pay, and I must pay it."

Only now, he went to his hut. There, in a corner, he discovered his bow and some arrows. He picked them up and left.

That night, Kanu went to the bungalow of the thekedar. He was alone, and he was sitting there drinking.

"We meet again," he challenged the contractor, pointing his arrow.

The thekedar tried to reach for his pistol. But an arrow from Kanu's bow prevented him. His right hand was pierced by the arrow.

Then he carefully aimed at the thekedar's heart.

"Don't–listen to me–I'll give you whatever compensation you want–much, much money–any amount you want."

These were his last words. The next moment the arrow shot out of Kanu's bow and got him in the heart.

He vomited blood.

He died instantly.

Kanu retrieved his two arrows, wiped them clean on the thekedar's clothes, then walked out.

Back at the hut of Kallo, the neighbor of Rambha.

"Give me my child. Now I am worthy of taking him in my lap!"

She gave him his child.

But she tried to make one last appeal to him.

"Kanu, don't go. Stay with me."

"No, Kallo, now I am an outlaw."

"Then take me with you!" I will be a second Rambha to you. She was my friend. I will go wherever you go, do whatever you do, cook for you, and serve you. Please."

"No Kallo, now that Rambha is gone—I'll walk alone!"

And he left, his son on his shoulder!

The forest swallowed them.

The zamindar's face seemed to have been cast in stone, with fierce moustache, pock-marks. Behind him hung a tiger-skin on the wall. He was smoking a hookah.

"What is it?" asked the zamindar.

The oily face of the zamindar's henchman, sparkled with flattery.

"*Huzoor*," he said, "they are refusing to harvest the fields."

"Who are refusing?" the zamindar asked.

"The tribal peasants," the henchman replied, "They want a wage of four rupees per day."

"Who has instigated them?" There was a challenge in the zamindar's voice.

There was fear in the hechman's whisper, "A Naxalite named Kanu Santhal, *Huzoor*."

"Tell them," commanded the zamindar, "we will get men from some other place to harvest our fields."

The henchman replied with folded hands, "*Huzoor*, they say it is their right. They will not let anyone else come to their territory."

The aristocrat exploded, "Nonsense! Tell them we are not afraid. Tell them we will see them ourselves." And he got up to go out.

"*Huzoor*–don't come out–they are too many–and they are in a temper–"

The zamindar drew himself to his full height, "We are not afraid of their temper–moreover we will have our gun and there will be cartridges in both the barrels."

The zamindar came out of the room into the *dalaan* of his mansion where the tribals were collected in the courtyard. They were talking among themselves.

As the zamindar came out, there was silence among the tribals.

"What is it I hear?" he demanded.

There was no reply from the tribals, utter silence.

"So you want four rupees a day?" the zamindar further asked in a thundering, commanding tone.

Once again there was utter silence.

"Speak up, men," he challenged, "What do you want? Or you dare not talk?"

An arrow came and got embedded in the door. There was a slip of paper along with it!

The zamindar was visibly shaken by the sudden arrival of the arrow. His servant removed the paper.

"Bhola!" said the zamindar, "What is written on the paper?"

Bhola (reading the paper) replied, "Four rupees a day—or we don't work. And we won't allow others to work in our place! Signed: Kanu Santhal."

Suddenly life surged through the ranks of the tribals who shouted in a defiant chorus. "We won't work. We won't work."

"Then, get out!" shouted the zamindar.

And the tribals got out—but not meekly.

"Bhola!" ordered the zamindar, "Go to Kaalnagri—and bring a hundred peasants. We will pay them two rupees per day."

Three trucks full of poor peasants came along the road walking at full speed, towards the zamindar's fields.

Tribal women and tribal men were standing. Among them was Kanu in the fields. The men were armed with bows and arrows, while women had rakhis and bangles on their hands.

Kanu spoke, standing on a height, "All the men—hide in the fields with your bows and arrows. Only the women will remain outside to talk to the blacklegs. If they break the women's lines and advance towards the fields, they will meet with our bows and arrows. No one is to shoot an arrow till I raise the cry '*Inquilab Zindabad*'. Understand, all of you?"

"Yes—yes," the tribal men responded, "We will hide in the crop!" Then they all went and hid in the crop including Kanu who was ahead of others.

The women remained at the boundaries of the fields.

The three trucks arrived on the scene.

As they stopped, an arrow (fired by Kanu) was imbedded in the side of the first truck. Then the women advanced offering their rakhis to the newcomers.

"Wear these rakhis brothers," said the women.

"But," a peasant protested, "it is not the day of Raksha Bandhan."

"It is our Raksha Bandhan, brother. We will make you our brothers so that you may protect your sisters."

One of the men replied, "But they said our men have all gone away to the city of work in the mills. Or why should they get men from a distant village?"

"Our men are all here–and you will meet them when the time comes," replied a woman, "But first wear these rakhis."

The zamindar's servants tried to stop the men but in vain.

But the blacklegs all surged forward offering their wrists to the womenfolk.

A man's wrist was decorated with a rakhi by a tribal woman– then all the men had the rakhis.

Just then the men with bows and arrows came out of the fields.

The two parties of men embraced each other.

Kanu also embraced the leader of the other peasants.

High above, the monsoon clouds were split by a rainbow of happiness.

12

WHY ARE YOU WEEPING, DEATH?

There are many worlds within this world. There are the prisons, on the iron gates of which may be inscribed: "Abandon hope, along with your clothes, all ye who enter here."

Within this world without hope, that is a prison, is another world which contains the death cells—where condemned prisoners spend the last few days of their life. The difference between an ordinary man (or woman) and a condemned prisoner is that the ordinary man does not know when exactly he will die, while the condemned prisoner knows the day, the hour and the minute of his (or her) death.

Seldom are the sounds of life—like the refrain of a song—heard in these death cells. But this night a woman's voice was singing, a Bengali below, the song "*Ek bar bidai de ma, ghuray ashi; Aami hashi hashi porobo phansi, dekhbay jagat-bashi.*"

It was the Naxalite girl Ajitha's death cell, and she was looking out through the barred window. The sky was starless and as dark as her own future. There was a clatter and the rattle of chains heard from the corridor, and Ajitha saw an iron plate with two chapattis inserted through the little space between the barred door. She went to the door, greeted the woman-warder with a "*Namaste, Chachi*" and a wistful smile.

The warder, notoriously a hard-hearted woman, burst into tears at the sight of a smile on the face of Ajitha who had only a few hours more to live.

"You are smiling, Ajitha," she said between sobs, "I have brought you your last meal."

"Thank you, *Chachi*. You have been very kind."

The female warder hid her face in the *anchal* of her sari as Ajitha sat down to have her last meal.

Across the barrier of iron bars from the women's ward of condemned cells were the condemned cells of the men.

In the first one of them, which had only a stone wall dividing it from Ajitha's cell, was the cell in which Haibat Khan, notorious Pathan strongman, was passing the last two days of his life.

At the moment, he was standing on an inverted bucket and engaged in the act of bending the bars with his bare strong hands. He would have bent the bars sufficiently to make a dangerous bid for a getaway but, at the last moment, he was apprehended and arrested–by a woman's voice.

Haibat Khan had an old weakness for women, he either loved them or hated them. For instance, he loved his mother, while he hated his wife–or hated her while he killed her, throttled her with own hands when he suspected her of infidelity. He was, or considered himself, a man of honour, and in his tribal world the punishment of a woman who betrayed her husband was death. That the charge of infidelity was, later, proved to be false was besides the point. He confessed to having killed her, for in his home village it was no crime to kill your wife who had proved–or whom you suspected–of being faithless. Too late he was convinced of her innocence. Meanwhile, he was sentenced to death. There were no mitigating circumstances, and the mercy petition, in view of his own confession, seemed like a lawyer's last desparate trick to make some more money. So Haibat Khan was to die the day after tomorrow–a day later than Ajitha. They would have died together but the hangman who needed a bottle of country liquor immediately after each hanging would not agree to two hangings in a day.

He had heard of Ajitha, who too had committed a crime of passion–of killing the boy she loved. He knew nothing of a Naxalite's motives. But that created a kinship between the two. They had killed the persons each of them loved, and now they were going to suffer the death penalty.

But Haibat Khan, despite his huge bulky frame was mortally afraid of Death. He was afraid of God and what punishment awaited him in the afterlife for having killed an innocent woman. In his life he had lied and gambled and squeezed money from poor workers, and he knew that each of these sins was punishable with brimstone and the fires of Hell. He did not want to die. He wanted to prolong the agony of life as much as he could.

That was why he wanted to make one desperate bid to escape from the death cell. If he was caught, then too he would be hanged. It gave him some sort of grim satisfaction, to contemplate that, now whatever he did or did not do, nothing worse than death awaited him. So why not? He strained at the bars–he almost separated them from their foundations–when his attention was distracted by a feminine voice–the voice of Ajitha raised in song, in a strange and unfamiliar language. He knew she was going to die in the morning. Still she was singing. Was she mad? A curiosity about the strange young woman gripped him—which overcame even his overpowering desire to escape.

He straightened the bent bars and came down from the overturned pail—his precarious perch.

He came to the door where he found Kalia, an old warder, with ferocious moustaches, whose good conduct was rewarded not only with remittance of the death penalty but with the prison-warder's post. Kalia, too, seemed tense—he was always tense on the eve of a hanging. So, seeing the Pathan standing at the door, he found an excuse to engage him in conversation.

"*Kaho,* Khan Saheb"—he was always polite to condemned prisoners on the eve of their hanging, "All is well, I hope."

"All is not well—in two days, I am to die—that girl over there (indicating the women's ward) is to die in a few hours, yet she is singing. Is she mad?"

"No, maybe she is singing some *bhajan*—it is not rare."

"But I hear that she does not believe in God but in some bearded fellow called *Kaal Markus.*"

"Then, maybe, she is singing to this god of hers. Everybody needs some god or the other to remember in the last hours of life."

"To me she seems crazy!" declared the Pathan as Kalia the warder departed on his rounds.

The Pathan came to the wall dividing the two cells. He knew there were cracks in it. From these cracks the song had percolated to his cell. Through these cracks, they could converse.

"Hey, sister—" he hissed.

"Yes, brother," she replied.

"You are not afraid?"

"Afraid of what?"

"Afraid of—d—death!" He was too scared to mention that name. "You can sing at such a time!"

"I was not singing–I was only reciting an old Bengali poem."

"What were you saying? I don't know Bengali very much, though I have lived for many years in Calcutta."

"I was saying to my mother–Give me *Al-vidah*, mother, and I promise to come again. Happily I will mount the gallows and the people of the whole world will see this spectacle!"

"Will you mount the gallows happily, sister?"

"I hope so, Khan Saheb, for with my death, Revolution will live."

"What is *re-bo-lu-shan*?" He could not understand in word.

"The 'Great Turning Over'. When the sky will descend to the earth, and the earth will reach the sky. The mighty will tumble and fall, and the lowly will come into their own. That process is called revolution."

The Pathan loudly reflected for some moments, "Then there would be no thieves and no robbers. No infidelity because of suspicion of love–of money. No murder and no murderers?"

"No, brother, in a truly revolutionary society, all these things will disappear."

"You call me brother. I am an ignorant, illiterate man. I hear you are an educated woman. Yet would call me brother–while you know I am a murderer."

"All men are our brothers. And I am a murderer too."

"Why did you kill?"

"I was told it was necessary, for *our* revolution."

"Our brothers? Our revolution? Are there others also like you!"

"Yes–hundreds and thousands of them all over the country."

"Then listen carefully, sister. I am going to escape. Once I am outside, I can break your bars too, and help you to escape. Then we can go together where your brothers are working for revolution."

"No, thanks, brother! Now it is too late for me. I don't want to spoil our reputation and our image by escaping from jail at the last moment. I have been sentenced to die. I have also refused to send a mercy petition to the president! I don't want the world to think that a Naxalite can be a coward, can be afraid of death!"

"You are what? What did you say? I am an ignorant man, sister."

"A Naxalite."

"What is that?"

"Naxalite literally means one who comes from Naxalbari! It is a village in North Bengal. But now it means one who believes in the 'Great Turning Over' which began in Naxalbari—one who is not afraid to die!"

"But I was afraid to die, I, the mighty Haibat Khan...after hearing you, I am not afraid to die."

"But you will escape?"

"Yes, I will."

"Then can you do something—not for me—but for the revolution!"

"I will do anything."

"Then you will have to go to the border of Bengal and Bihar. There, in the jungle of Balaranga, our party is going to have a meeting. There I want you to give them a message from me—Ajitha Chatterjee—to my comrades."

"I will certainly do it. What shall I say?"

"Tell them I was not afraid to die. I will be dead tomorrow morning. I will write the message for you."

"What will you write with? There is no ink and no paper."

"I will write it with my blood. And I will write it on a piece of my prison costume. You must take it through the bars as I pass your cell door on my way to the gallows. Will you deliver it?"

"Yes, I swear by Allah, I will, sister."

On his face shone the great revelation. It was like a new light—a new music of the soul's awakening.

Ajitha's last moment had arrived. After a bath, for which a pail of water was brought, she combed her hair carefully, then she was handcuffed but in her hand she had hidden a piece of cloth. Then a procession was formed. The jailer led it. Then came the jail doctor. Then a priest. After that two very tall policemen, then Ajitha, then two more tall policemen, each carrying a bayoneted rifle.

The door of the women's ward was unlocked and the procession paused in front of Haibat Khan's cell.

"*Khuda hafiz, bahen,*" said Haibat Khan loudly.

"*Namaste*, Khan Saheb," and, as she folded her handcuffed hands, she passed the little piece of cloth to the Pathan. The tall policemen were too tall—and looking ahead stiffly—to see what had transferred between the short condemned woman and the burly Pathan.

After she had passed out of the gate in the courtyard of the prison where the gallows had been set up, the gate was closed.

During this time the Pathan got an opportunity to break his bars and make his escape.

Through the broken bars the sun was rising in all its glory.

13

MESSAGE FROM THE GALLOWS!

In a thick jungle where no human habitation was visible.

A Marxist-Leninist Party flag hung from a barren tree. There was not a soul to be seen anywhere.

Slowly, to the rhythm of distant drums, people started arriving, singing the Internationale.

They were identified by their footwear—or lack of footwear.

Peasants with bare, calloused, feet.

Farmers in desi *jootis*.

Maharashtrians in Kolhapuri chappals.

Rajasthanis in their characteristic shoes.

Intellectuals with ragged regular shoes and shorts.

Fleet boots, rubber shoes.

Most of them were wearing shorts, ready for running.

By the evening, thirty thousand of them had arrived.

Their passes had been scrutinised.

There was place enough to sit on the ground—the jungle trees provided them shade.

People had walked great distances.

They had come by train.

By buses.

But the last few miles they had walked from all sides.

Under the red flag a portrait was installed—the portrait of Mao Tse-tung.

The arrivers were squatting on the ground and unpacking parcels of food which they had brought with them.

Dry chapatties.

Onions.

Potatoes.

Chillies.

Balls of rice.

The food of the proletariat bound to the waist and the belly of the proletariat.

No sophistication.

No ostentation.

Tough men—toughened by their experiences.

Ready to kill and be killed.

With arms.

Muzzle-loading guns.

Handmade grenades.

Country-made revolvers.

Army revolvers snatched from policemen.

Bows and arrows of tribals like Kanu Santhal—who was carrying his son on his shoulder.

Some checkposts had been established—at a distance of half a mile from each other. With drums to beat in case of a sudden police raid—one would give the alarm—and the next one would transmit it to the next one and so on—till the people gathered were warned.

At sunset, the meeting was started.

Comrade Dada began-.

"Comrades—

"Comrades steeled in the fire of Telangana.

"Comrades with the revolutionary traditions of Bengal who gave the name to our party by their historic action in Naxalbari.

"Comrades from the Punjab of Sardar Bhagat Singh.

"Comrades from Kerala whose Vylar showed the way to us even in the days of darkness of feudal rule.

"Comrades from everywhere.

"From Uttar Pradesh of Chandrashekhar Azad.

"From Gujrat.

"From Maharashtra of–

"You the landless labourers from all provinces–

"From the tribal belt all the way from the foothills of the Himalayas to the burning plains of Madhya Pradesh.

"You are not YOU!

"Each of you is a torch lit in the cause of REVOLUTION.

"You are representative of the anger and indignation of the 600 million people of this land of ours.

"We do not worship Mother India.

"To us each peasant woman who gives birth to a sturdy child and rears him to be a revolutionary–is Mother India.

"To you all.

"LAL SALAM!"

A roar of 30,000 voices echoed the greeting "*Lal Salam*".

After the chorus of voices died down, a burly Pathan got up to speak.

"*Lal Salam*, comrades!" Everyone looked at him for he was unknown.

"You don't know me–three months ago I was not a Naxalite."

"I was just a common murderer–who happened to be in the next death cell to your comrade. She died on the gallows, a revolutionary to the end till her voice was choked, but before she died she converted me to the cause of revolution. I was to die the next day but I am alive today to deliver a message that she sent you. She had no paper, so she wrote it on a piece of her prison dress. Here it is. Her name must be well known to you. It was AJITHA."

From all over came shouts of "*Ajitha Zindabad!*"

The Pathan handed the torn and faded cloth with the red letters scrawled over it—and the leader read it aloud:

> "Comrades, think what you are doing. You have killed enough—and sufficient number of you have been killed. Some at hands of Naxalites. Think whether it has led us to the goal of revolution. Not MURDER, but mass awakening, mass organisation, is the way to revolution. I am not afraid to die. You asked me to kill and I killed—even the one I loved! You asked me to die and I am dying—but from the threshold of death I am sending this message to you to reconsider your methods. Goodbye. And *Lal Salam*."

There was pindrop silence as the message was read out.

Comrade Dada did not agree with the message of Ajitha.

"This is sabotage—this man has been sent as a spy. What proof is there that this is really Ajitha's message? Our comrade could never be a coward—"

On the word "coward", the burly Pathan flared up.

"Coward? You dare to call her a coward? I have never seen a braver woman than her. She was an angel who transformed a useless man like me into something by her mere voice and her courage. You dare to call her a coward! She who died so that the revolution might live."

For a fraction of a second there was silence, then the cry in chorus arose. "*Ajitha Zindabad! Ajitha Zindabad!*" The cry went from one group to another till it was as if it came from the whole country.

One man, a peasant from Telengana, arose. "I propose that we reconsider our plan and programme in view of Comrade Ahitha's message."

Another man from Bengal arose, "Comrades, individual terrorism won't do. We must organise the poor, landless labour for revolutionary action. This is how all revolutions were successful."

Yet another man from the Punjab, arose, "People mistake us for common murderers. We must remove this impression."

A dark fellow from Kerala rose. "Enough of individual terrorism. We must revise our programmes, become a regular revolutionary party."

"Let us take part in the elections," said one.

"We will sweep the polls so far as the poor and the landless are concerned."

The tables were turned.

Comrade Dada was defeated.

From a distance, came the distant rumble of drumbeats.

Everyone listened.

"The police are coming."

"No panic!" said Comrade Dada. "Let the people go in silence the way they came. There is no way out of the web of violence. You may be non-violent but will the police be non-violent? We will not fire the first shot."

The same drummer came running, breathless.

"The police will be here in about half an hour."

"Enough time for the people to disperse. The hardcore of the party, the armed men with their weapons will hold the post and keep the police at bay. That will give our comrades enough time to escape.

The thirty thousand people silently withdrew in a disciplined manner.

Forty or fifty men took positions on the top of the hill behind barricades of trees and branches.

Soon the police vans arrived.

The first shot was fired by the police.

"Just as I said."

There was a volley of fire aimed at the police.

EPILOGUE

When the police had killed every Naxalite, the DIG shouted, "Is there a Naxalite alive?"

Three times he repeated the question after raining the dead bodies with a shower of bullets.

Kanu Santhal's dead body received some more bullets–but saved his son hidden behind it.

"Is there a Naxalite alive?" spoke the voice of the police officer through a microphone.

"If there is, let him come out with his two hands raised above his head. Otherwise he too will be killed."

There was a stirring behind the dead body of Kanu Santhal.

There was the paleness of dawn in the sky.

The police officer aimed the revolver, ready to shoot.

But out came the child, from behind his father's lifeless body.

Kanu Santhal's four-year-old son, Surya, holding his hands up–the sole surviving Naxalite, calling out, "My name is SURYA!"

Against the glowing dawn he became frozen into a symbol of innocence and defiance–the symbol of Revolution–and that was THE BEGINNING!

ABBAS ON NAXALITES

"Since the cinema is a director's medium, it is his creative vision and his decision that must be supreme and final. I venture to hope that in the original literary form it may interest some readers, not as the story of the film but as the story on which the film was based. The intelligent readers may also get an insight into the creative process by which a competent film-maker transforms a story into a film, translates the author's word pictures into cinematic images, how and where and why deviations are made, for instance, to accommodate songs and dances.

"Human destiny in its social setting has been my special preoccupation–some may call it my obsession. Whether doing my weekly column, writing short stories and novels, scripting screenplays for other producers, or writing, directing and producing my own films, I have been involved with the themes of social transformation and social justice.

"I had, meanwhile, completed my film, *Naxalites*, and was invited to International Festival of Neo-Realistic Films in the village of Avellino in Italy, for which Dr Singal gave me immediate permission and good wishes. So I started for Italy, along with Sumit Mukherjee the hero of my *Naxalites* whom I had brought from Calcutta but who stubbornly refused to learn Hindi, and so he could not get any other good role except playing the Bengali character in *Naxalites.*

"Since there are any number of my Indian and Pakistani friends and relations in London, I got my ticket routed via London from where I proceeded to Brussels to meet my friend, Mrs Marie Jose Berguin, her husband Jackues and their child Razia, whom they had adopted from a Christian 'home' in India several years ago and who has developed into a dusky but beautiful young French speaking girl on whom both her foster parents simply doted. After a brief stop in Brussels, we returned to London and after attending several literary gatherings of Urdu writers, mushairas and story-readings, we were ready to return to Italy.

"In Rome, we had a 'home away from home' in the flat of India's First Secretary where we were made perfectly at home. We saw the immense Coliseum, including the lions' cages and the Gladiators' room where Spartacus enacted the life and death drama of life, refusing to kill *his* friend and being beheaded in reprisal by the Caesar. Next day we went to see the Sisteen Chapel, the masterpiece of which was itself worth a visit to Rome. Since I had missed it on my first visit to Rome in 1938 when I had to leave in a hurry because there was a premature rumour of war having started or about to start that day, and so we piled into a train which was full to capacity and we had to stand in the narrow corridor, all the way to France.

"The next day we started for Avellino, the village where the Festival of Neo-Realistic Films was to be held. The bus off-loaded us in the village square. There were no taxis, so we had to carry our baggage on our own shoulders to the main hotel which accommodated the office of the Festival Committee. After a cup of coffee we were told there was no room left in the little hotel and we were given room in the hotel at the other end of the village (or town). A friendly festival official volunteered to take us there in his car, and we found our friend Devendra Kumar, editor of Delhi's *Time* and *Tide* already there, waiting for us.

"From that onwards, it became my schedule twice a day to walk (or hobble) two miles to the Festival Cinema in the morning and evening. There were some good neo-realistic films from countries – from USSR, USA, France, Hungry, Yugoslavia, Italy, Germany, Great Britain, Holand, Belgium, etc. etc.

"Our *Naxalites* was certainly among the top contenders for a big award. This I gathered from the packed house that turned up for the screening and stayed on to question me elaborately. Then I knew that urban guerillas as 'Red Guards' were active in Italy, too. Comparisons between 'Naxalites' and 'Red Guards' were obviously made, and I was asked which party had financed my picture. I replied 'None' which surprised the audience because in their country 'Red Guards' would naturally finance such a picture. They have known to have amassed millions of Lire from banks and capitalists. Naxalites are generally rural based, therefore, they are not rich with so much money. 'But we doubt if any Italian producer would take up the case of the 'Red Guards' for filming,' one of the audience said, 'But, Mr Abbas, you have made a nice picture which deserves a big award,' he concluded.

"Thus it was not surprising for me to hear the announcement that I had won the Gold Prize for direction and was to share it with a Russian director, who had made a neo-realistic film with ten times the financial resources that I had.

"I returned from Italy with the Gold Award and a lame foot."

The above excerpt has been taken from K.A. Abbas's interview to the Indian Literary Review

About the Author

Khwaja Ahmad Abbas (1914-87) was a prolific political commentator, short story writer, novelist, scriptwriter and a film maker who preferred to call himself a communicator. He published 73 books in English, Hindi and Urdu, including an engaging autobiography, and two semi-autobiographical novels, *Inquilab* and *The World is My Village* detailing contemporary history. His works have been translated into several Indian and foreign languages. Amongst the earliest of art and socially relevant cinema his films include *Saat Hindustani* in which he gave a break to Amitabh Bachchan, *Faslah* with which Shabana Azmi made her debut, and *The Naxalite* that starred the erstwhile real-life Naxalite, Mithun Chakravorty opposite Smita Patil.

Suresh Kohli (born in 1947) is a poet, writer, translator, editor, literary critic and film historian with more than 35 published works including five volumes of poetry and a novel. He is also a short and documentary film-maker, with over a hundred films to his credit that have been screened, apart from India, in Australia, France, Germany, Spain, the United Kingdom and Nepal. He is presently in Delhi and is working on a long abandoned novel and a collection of short stories.